BABYSITTERS' ISLAND ADVENTURE

"Hey! You lot!" yelled Claudia. "Stay with us! You keep drifting away!"

"Our rudder's broken!" I shouted. "And our boat's filling up with water."

It was at that point, as I noticed Claudia's torch bobbing away, that Jeff, trying not to sound frightened, crossed the boat and tried to whisper to me (which was not easy), "We're sinking."

"We're what?" I'd heard him, but I didn't want to believe him.

"We're sinking," he repeated quietly.

Claudia and Dawn have planned the perfect day-trip—a sailing race to Greenpoint Island. Then a storm blows up and they're shipwrecked on an island with four kids. What will happen to the Babysitters Club if two of their members are missing—for good?

BABYSITTERS' ISLAND ADVENTURE

Ann M. Martin

Hippo Books
Scholastic Publications Limited
London

Scholastic Children's Books
Scholastic Publications Ltd,
7–9 Pratt Street, London NW1 0AE, UK

Scholastic Inc.,
730 Broadway, New York, NY 10003, USA

Scholastic Canada Ltd,
123 Newkirk Road, Richmond Hill,
Ontario, Canada L4C 3G5

Ashton Scholastic Pty Ltd,
P O Box 579, Gosford, New South Wales,
Australia

Ashton Scholastic Ltd,
Private Bag 1, Penrose, Auckland,
New Zealand

First published in the US by Scholastic Inc., 1990
First published in the UK by Scholastic Publications Limited, 1992

ISBN 0 590 55017 9

THE BABY-SITTERS CLUB is a trademark of Scholastic Inc.

Typeset in Plantin by Contour Typesetters, Southall, London
Printed by Cox & Wyman Ltd, Reading, Berks

10 9 8 7 6 5 4 3 2 1

*This book is for
the mascots of the Lunch Club:
Kathryn and Michael,
Christian and Callie*

I thought finding the secret passage in my house was exciting. I thought going on a cruise through the Bahamas and then visiting Disney World was exciting. I thought sneaking into a graveyard on Hallowe'en night was exciting.

I thought my parents' divorce was traumatic. I thought moving from sunny California to snowy (in the winter) Connecticut in the middle of a school year was traumatic. I thought getting a stepfather and stepsister was traumatic (and exciting).

I was right about everything— but that was before my friend Claudia Kishi and I got stranded on an island with four children. Now that was exciting and traumatic! I still can't believe it happened. Claudia and I set out on a sailing adventure with my younger brother, Jeff, and three kids we sometimes baby-sit for — Haley Braddock, who's nine; Becca Ramsey, who's eight; and Jamie Newton, who's just four. We never thought our dream trip would turn into a nightmare.

But it did.

Haley said the adventure was a bit like being in one of her favourite books, <u>Baby Island</u>, by Carol Ryrie Brink. In that book, two girls are travelling on an ocean liner that gets shipwrecked, and the girls end up in a lifeboat with four babies and have to live on a tropical island for ages before they're rescued. At least Claudia and I didn't have to take care of any babies. A lively eight-year-old, a nine-year-old, my brother, and Jamie were enough. And at least we didn't have to wait <u>too</u> long to be rescued, although I must admit that the length of time we were on the island seemed like an eternity.

While we're talking about books, I should also mention that <u>Jeff</u>

said the adventure was a bit like being in a book he'd read in school that year. The book is called The Cay, and it's by Theodore Taylor. I read it once, too. I'm glad our experience wasn't as harrowing (or as long) as the boy's was in that book. Still...

My adventure was the best and the worst thing that ever happened to me. (So far. I'm only thirteen. I assume that better and worse things will happen if I live long enough to let them.)

Since being stranded on the island was so exciting and traumatic, I decided I wanted to have a record of it. Of course, no one ever expects to get stranded on an island after a sailing trip, so I didn't have a pen or any paper with me. In order to have a record of the experience, I had to rely on my friends' memories, letters, diaries, and notes from the time I was away, and also,

3

of course, on Claudia's and my memories. As soon as we got home, we tried to write down everything we could remember. For Claudia, this wasn't an easy job, since she's the world's worst speller and doesn't like to write. She did it anyway, though, which just goes to show what a good friend she is.

Also, when we were back, safe and sound, in good old Stoneybrook, Connecticut, I interviewed my friends. That was fun. Maybe I'll be a reporter one day.

I haven't thought of a better career.

Anyway, thanks to help from members of the Babysitters Club — Kristy Thomas, Jessi Ramsey, Stacey McGill, Mallory Pike, Mary Anne Spier (my _best_ friend), and Claudia, my co-disaster victim, I managed to write about the whole adventure, even the parts that didn't take place on the island. In fact, even the parts that took place in New York City, which, by the way, doesn't seem as exciting a place as a deserted island just now.

So... here goes my story.

— Dawn Schafer

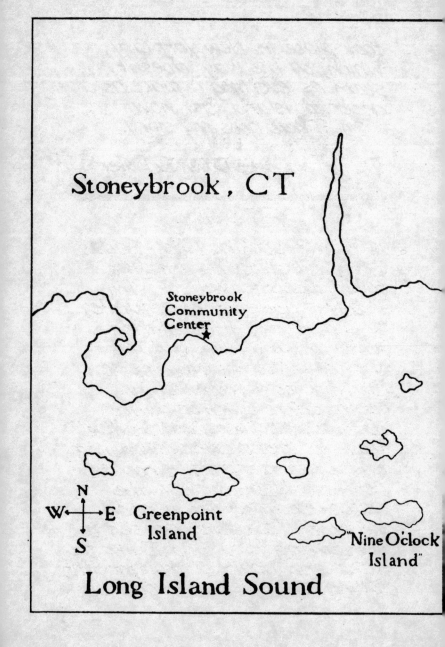

1st CHAPTER

Dawn

Looking Back-Friday

It all started with the sailing lessons. Well, if I'm really going to be accurate, I should say it all started when Mallory Pike told me that as well as everything else Stoneybrook's community centre offers (such as dance classes, art lessons, and creative theatre), it also offers swimming and boating classes, since the centre is located near the water. Because I'm a good swimmer (I've even passed a life-saving test) and I like the water and boats, I thought that taking sailing lessons would be

7

fun. I'd been sailing before —
lots of times, in fact. So had Claudia
Kishi. So we signed up for
sailing classes at the community
centre If we hadn't, we would
never have had our adventure.

"Well, are you ready?" I asked.

"Am I ready? I'm going to beat you hollow!" replied Claudia.

We were on the phone, and we'd challenged each other to a sailing race, which would be held the next day.

"No, you're not. I did tons of sailing with Dad and Jeff when I lived in California. And we go sailing almost every time I visit them now."

My parents are divorced. Mum and I live here in Stoneybrook, and Dad and Jeff live in California. Why? That's a long story. To make it short, let me just say that Mum grew up in Stoneybrook, but she met my father in California, where *he'd* grown up. After the divorce, it seemed natural for Mum to go back to Connecticut with Jeff and me. But Jeff never adjusted to things here, so he went back to Dad and California, where he'd always been happy. I visit them whenever I can.

"Well, I sail every summer when we go away on holiday," said Claudia. "Let's face it. You and I are pretty evenly matched. We've been

8

taking lessons from the same instructors for two months now."

"You're right. Tomorrow will be a close race. . . . But I'm still going to beat you!" I replied.

"I wish the instructors would let us race to Greenpoint on our own, without helpers," said Claudia. "I don't want the helpers any more." (Greenpoint is an island off the coast where the community centre often holds special events.)

"I don't want the helpers either. They're nice, but having them with us is a bit of a drag. It's like going clothes shopping with your parents."

"Besides, we've sailed to Greenpoint a million times." (That was an exaggeration, naturally.)

"I know," I said.

"I suppose they're afraid we'll go off course. There *are* an awful lot of teeny, tiny islands all up and down the coast."

"Really?"

"Of course." (Claud knows Connecticut much better than I do, since she grew up here and I'm a recent transplant.) "Some of them are so small that people *own* them. Imagine owning an island! They look like pinpricks from up in an aeroplane. There must be hundreds of them." (This time, I knew Claud wasn't exaggerating.)

"Wow!" I said.

"Anyway, get ready for Greenpoint," said Claud. "I'm going to bed now. I want to rest before the big race."

Rest? Ha! Claud just wanted a chance to go to bed early. She likes to get under the covers with a good Nancy Drew mystery. And, possibly, a bar of chocolate.

On the other hand, I was going to exercise, fill up with some pasta, and get a normal amount of sleep. *That* was the way to win the race—wasn't it?

The next morning—Saturday—I woke up at seven-thirty. I exercised some more. Then I ate a healthy breakfast. I felt fit. I knew I was ready for the race. And I was pretty sure I could beat Claudia.

"You've got great racing weather," said Mary Anne.

Mary Anne isn't just my best friend. She's my stepsister, too. My mum isn't single any more. After we moved to Connecticut, Mum fell in love with—you won't believe this!—an old boyfriend from schooldays. He happened to be the father of the first friend I made in Stoneybrook—Mary Anne Spier. And not long ago, Mum and Richard (that's Mary Anne's father, who was a widower) got married. Isn't that romantic? Then Richard, Mary Anne, and Tigger (Mary Anne's kitten) moved into our house.

"We've got perfect weather," I said to Mary Anne. "Just perfect."

"Your mum and my dad and I are going to see

you off," Mary Anne went on. "We'll be there for the finish, too. But I think I'll come home in between."

I could understand why. Mary Anne has super-sensitive skin. She gets as red as a lobster after about half an hour in the sun. And Greenpoint Island, the place Claudia and I were going to race to and from, is almost three miles out in Long Island Sound. There was no way Mary Anne could stand around in the sun for a six-mile race.

"That's okay," I told her. As I mentioned before, Mary Anne and I understand each other.

Two hours later, Richard was driving our family to the community centre.

"You know," said Mary Anne, "I really hope you win."

I almost asked why she *wouldn't* want her own sister to win. But instead I just said, "Thanks."

"I wouldn't mind if Claud won, though," she went on.

"You *what*?"

(Richard glanced at us in the rearview mirror.)

"Well, it's just—you know." (Mary Anne lowered her voice.) "Claudia's school report." We get reports several times a year.

"What about it?" I asked.

"It wasn't very good. I think she's feeling

11

pretty bad about herself at the moment. If she won the race, she might feel better."

"That's true," I said slowly, thinking it over.

"At least her parents didn't make her drop out of the Babysitters Club," Mary Anne pointed out. (They're always threatening to do that. The BSC is a business that my friends and I run. We babysit for families in our neighbourhoods.)

"Yes," I agreed.

We drove the rest of the way to the community centre in silence. When we arrived, the first person I saw was Claudia, and she certainly looked ready to race—and win.

"Good luck!" called Mum and Richard and Mary Anne. They joined a crowd of other people who were standing on the quay. Claudia's parents and sister were there, and so were the rest of our friends in the BSC, as well as Logan Bruno, who's Mary Anne's steady boyfriend (and also an associate member of the club), and a few interested kids and some people from the centre.

The race started off well (for me) since I was in the lead. I'd dressed properly for sailing—loose, comfortable clothes I could move around in, and that wouldn't get caught in anything. Claudia, on the other hand, couldn't help dressing up just a little. She's a real clotheshorse, and I suppose she wanted to look good, since she knew we'd have an audience. So she'd put on a tank top and baggy draw-string trousers. Over the top, she was

12

wearing one of her father's shirts. The sleeves were rolled up, but none of the buttons were fastened. She was also wearing big earrings she'd made herself. Claudia's quite artistic. So the thing is, she *looked* good but, as it turned out, she wasn't dressed for sailing.

As soon as we were on the water and had picked up some speed, her shirt started blowing around. She spent more time peeling the shirt off her face than steering the boat or doing anything else. *Then* one of her huge earrings got caught on a sail and she had to struggle to set it free. With the wind blowing around me, I couldn't hear anything from her boat, but I could see her lips moving and I bet she was saying some things she isn't supposed to say. Anyway, the helper took her earrings off for her, and Claudia buttoned up her shirt. Still, I reached Greenpoint before she did.

I lost no time turning round and heading back, but this time the wind had changed direction, and I had trouble steering.

Uh-oh! I thought. Claudia's going to catch up. Sure enough, the closer we got to the community centre, the closer Claudia got to *me*. By the time the race was over . . . .

"Tie! It's a tie!" yelled Kristy Thomas from her place in the crowd.

Everyone agreed with her. Personally, I thought I was a couple of centimetres ahead of Claud at the end, but who am I to argue with twenty people, most of whom are my friends?

The only good thing that came of the race was that the head sailing instructor said Claud and I didn't need helpers with us any more. "No sailing *alone*," she cautioned, "but you don't need helpers."

"Thank you," Claud and I said politely, even though we both wanted to cheer.

Then Claudia challenged me to a replay. Of course, I accepted. If only I'd known what would happen when we raced again!

2nd CHAPTER

Mary Anne

Looking Back—
Monday

I don't usually record
what happens at a
meeting of the Baby-Sitters
Club. I just make
appointments for sitting
jobs. But when Dawn
decided she wanted to
write about her adventure,
I looked back at the
record book to see if I
could remember what
had happened at that
Monday BSC meeting
before Claud and Dawn's
replay.

It was two days after

the race, the race that Claudia almost lost due to earrings and bad dressing. Kristy was trying to conduct an official meeting, but all my stepsister and Claud could talk about was their race. Each thought she had won....

"It was just my earrings," complained Claud.

"And your shirt," Dawn couldn't help pointing out.

Claudia made a face. She's the vice-chairman of the Babysitters Club. Her job is . . . well, she's vice-chairman because she's got her own phone and personal, private phone number, so her room is the perfect place to hold our Monday, Wednesday, and Friday club meetings.

What *is* the Babysitters Club? Well, it's really a business. It's a group of girls (the seven that Dawn mentioned) who get together three times a week and arrange babysitting jobs. Our clients know we meet at these times because we do a lot of advertising. They phone us during meetings to arrange babysitters for their children.

Another reason Claud is the vice-chairman is that we invade her room three times a week. She provides us with snacks, if needed. Claudia is as

16

addicted to junk food as she is to Nancy Drew books, but since her parents don't approve of either habit, she has to hide both the food and the books all over her room. Claud lives with her parents and her older sister, Janine, who's a genius. This is a nuisance for Claud. She loves her sister, but it's not easy living with a genius when you're a bad pupil, even if you are clever. I wished Claud had got a better school report. I almost wished she'd win the replay. Then she'd feel better about herself. Sometimes Claudia thinks she's not good at *anything* except art and baby-sitting.

"Can we please get back to the matter in hand?" asked Kristy, sounding agitated. (She meant the meeting.) Kristy's chairman of the BSC, since it was her idea, and she's always getting lots of other ideas for keeping the club running—and running well. She tries to conduct the meetings in a businesslike manner, but that day she actually seemed cross. And I knew it wasn't because of us. Dawn's my best friend, and Kristy is my other best friend. I know her like the back of my hand. Something was wrong. Was it her family? Kristy lives in a big, mixed-up family with a stepfather, a stepbrother, a stepsister, an adopted sister, her grandmother, her mother and her brothers, not to mention two pets.

"Kristy?" I said tentatively. (I hate arguments and I cry easily.) "Is anything wrong?"

17

Mary Anne

"Oh . . ." Kristy sighed heavily. "I'm sorry. It's the Krushers." (The Krushers are the children on a softball team that Kristy organised and coaches.) "They're upset. We lost to the Bashers *again*. The children are getting a little disheartened. They think they'll never win a game. What they don't see is that they're getting better all the time. Maybe they'll win next Monday. We've got another game then."

We had a three-day weekend coming up, which we were all looking forward to as if we'd never had a holiday in our lives.

"Well, we'll come and cheer the Krushers on," said Stacey, our treasurer. It's her job to collect subs and handle money; to make sure we have enough in the treasury to help Claud pay her monthly phone bill, for instance. Stacey is Claudia's best friend, and it's easy to see why. The two of them are chic, sophisticated, and trendy. Stacey grew up in New York City. (She's so lucky. As soon as I'm old enough, I plan to move there.) But now she lives in Stoneybrook. Her parents got divorced recently, and her father still lives in the Big Apple, so Stacey goes to the city to visit him any weekend she wants. Lately she hasn't been going as often as usual, though. Stacey has diabetes and hasn't been feeling very well. I think her visits have turned into command performances. Her father says, "Come", and Stacey goes, whether she wants to or not.

"Thanks, Stacey," said Kristy, and at that moment, the phone rang. "Oh, goody! A job call!" she went on, her eyes brightening.

"I'll get it," said Dawn. Dawn is our alternative officer, which means she's a bit like a substitute teacher. She knows what's involved in being any officer of the club, and can take over that job if one of us has to miss a meeting. That doesn't give her much to do most of the time, though, so since Dawn likes to be busy, she answers the phone a lot.

"Hello, Babysitters Club," she said.

I got out the record book. I'm the club secretary and it's my duty to arrange babysitting jobs, and also to know everybody's timetable— when Kristy has a Krushers' practice or Mallory has a dental appointment or Jessi has a ballet class.

"Tuesday afternoon?" Dawn was saying. "I'll get right back to you, Mrs Prezzioso."

"Uh-oh!" I said, as Dawn rang off and everyone else began groaning—and hoping they were busy on Tuesday.

Jenny Prezzioso is a pain. (I'm sorry, but she is.) I'm really the only one who can stick her. Unfortunately, I wasn't free on Tuesday. But Mallory was. "It's your job," I told her.

"Great!" replied Mal sarcastically.

"Hey, junior officer," said Kristy. "That's what you're here for."

19

"I know, I know."

Mallory Pike and Jessi Ramsey are our junior officers because they're younger than the rest of us. They're eleven and in the sixth grade, and we're thirteen and in the eighth grade. (By the way, we all go to Stoneybrook Middle School, or SMS.) Mal and Jessi joined the club to give us a hand with afternoon jobs, since they're not allowed to babysit at night unless they're sitting for their own families.

Although Mal and Jessi come from different backgrounds and have very different families, they're best friends—and they do have some things in common. Here are the differences: Mallory is white, has *seven* younger brothers and sisters, wants to be a children's book author, and grew up in Stoneybrook. Jessi is black, has just one younger sister and a baby brother, is a talented dancer, and recently moved to Connecticut from New Jersey. Here are the similarities: both Mal and Jessi like to read, especially horse stories, and both feel that their parents treat them like babies. However, their parents are relaxing a little. They let their daughters get their ears pierced, Mal's parents let her get a new haircut, and—best of all—Jessi's parents were letting her look after Becca and Squirt (her sister and brother) all by herself for the whole of the holiday weekend. What a breakthrough!

Mallory reluctantly agreed to babysit for Jenny

20

Prezzioso on Tuesday. When that was arranged and the phone didn't ring for a while, Claudia brought up the replay again. It was a bit of an obsession with her.

"How about this Saturday?" she suggested. "This time *I am* going to win. What a way to start off the weekend!"

"This Saturday?" Dawn repeated slowly. "I don't know. Jeff's going to be visiting. He gets a *four*-day weekend at *his* school. I don't want to miss being—Hey, wait! Perhaps Jeff could come *with* me! We don't need helpers any more, but we're not allowed to sail alone."

"Well, then, *I've* got to get a crew member, too," said Claud. She looked at Mal. "How about it?"

I knew she was choosing Mallory because, except for her sister Margo, who gets seasick, the Pike family loves boating and they spend a lot of time on the water.

"I'd like to," Mal replied, looking flattered, "but Mum and Dad have got things planned for the weekend."

Jessi spoke up shyly. "I think Becca would *love* to go with you," she said. "She's hardly ever been on a boat, but she'd think it was really exciting. She's—she's been a bit jealous recently because of my dancing. She'd like to find something athletic—and different—that *she* could be good at. What do you think? She's a quick learner."

21

"I'd love to take Becca with me," Claud answered.

So Dawn rang her mother to get permission to hold the replay on Saturday and to ask if Jeff could sail with her. Then Jessi rang her parents and, even though they were frantically making last-minute plans for their weekend away, they said that Becca could go sailing with Claudia.

It was settled. My friends were going to hold their replay on Saturday— and they'd found crew members.

3rd CHAPTER

Dawn

Looking Back-Tuesday and Wednesday

By the next day, the day after our meeting, the replay had turned into more than just another race. It was to be an outing as well. All it took was a few phonecalls — to Jeff, who was still in California, to Becca, to Mr and Mrs Newton, and to Mr and Mrs Braddock.

"What a great day Saturday's going to be!" exclaimed Claudia.

As it turned out, she was half right. It started out as a great day, but the ending was... well, you'll see.

On Monday, Mum had agreed to Jeff being my crew member, but I thought I'd better check with him personally. What if he arrived on Friday and didn't want to go sailing for some reason? Then I'd have to scramble around for a new crew member. And if I couldn't find one, we'd have to reschedule the race, and Becca would be disappointed, and Claud would be upset. I wasn't really worrying. I was just covering all eventualities.

So on Monday night, I rang Jeff. The three-hour time difference between the East Coast and the West Coast is such a pain. I usually wait until 10 P.M. my time, knowing Jeff and Dad will probably be at home at 7 P.M. their time. I also usually interrupt their dinner.

Tuesday was no exception.

At ten on the dot, I picked up the phone and dialled my dad's house. Jeff answered. (He loves to answer the phone.) Usually, he answers it normally, but that night he said in a deep voice, "Hello, Marcel's Dry Cleaning."

I knew it was Jeff straight away, and started to giggle.

"Hey, you great berk!" I said affectionately. "You can't fool me. This is your sister. Who were you expecting? A friend of yours?"

Jeff lowered his voice. "No, Carol." (Carol's Dad's girlfriend. Jeff and I don't like her much, although I think she's growing on Jeff. But he still tries to cut her off from Dad sometimes.)

"Jeff! That's not nice."

"I know," he replied.

I couldn't help laughing.

"Do you want to talk to Dad?" asked my brother.

"Maybe in a few minutes. I want to talk to you first, though. It's about this weekend."

"Oh, no! It's off, isn't it? You've decided to go away or something, haven't you?"

"Of course not, silly. Claudia and I are having a sailing race on Saturday and I want to know if you'd like to be my crew member. We're sailing to Greenpoint Island and back." (Jeff had been there once before.) "Mum already said you could go," I added.

"Really? Great. I'll be there!"

"Terrific!"

I talked to Jeff a bit longer, and then to Dad, but Dad and I were interrupted when Carol dropped in.

Jeff got back on the phone. "The Hair Queen's here," he whispered.

I laughed again. Jeff's new nickname for Carol is the Hair Queen because she's always getting her hair cut or dyed or something.

When Jeff and I rang off, I rang Claud straight away.

"Hi!" she said.

25

"Hi!" I replied. "Well, Jeff's ready. He's really excited about the race."

"Great!" said Claud, "but we've got one tiny problem."

"What?"

"Becca's so excited about the race that she began ringing all her friends to tell them about it. Most of the children just thought the race sounded fun, but Haley Braddock wants to come with us."

The Braddocks are clients of the BSC. They've got two children—Haley, who's nine, and Matt, who's seven. Matt is profoundly deaf. That means that he really can't hear anything. And he can't talk. He goes to a school for the deaf in Stamford, and he communicates using sign language. All the Braddocks use sign language, even Haley. In fact, she's almost an expert. So she's a nice child, but I think sometimes she feels that Matt gets all the attention in her family. That was probably why she wanted to go boating so badly. It would be something special for *her*.

"Well, that *is* a problem," I agreed. "I'd hate to tell Haley she can't come with us when she wants an invitation so badly."

"I know . . ." replied Claud slowly. "But it's not fair for me to have two crew members and you to have only one, even though the children won't be doing much. In fact, having Becca and Haley

26

with me might even make me *lose*. They're both pretty inexperienced."

"How about this?" I suggested brightly. "You let Haley come, and I'll find a second crew member, too. One who's completely inexperienced, to make up for Jeff."

"Well . . . Who would you ask?"

I thought for a few moments. At last I said, "I know this sounds daft, but how about Jamie?"

"Jamie *Newton*?" cried Claud. "He's only four."

"I know, but he'd love it. He's a good swimmer —he's been taking lessons—and he has a thing about boats just now. They fascinate him. Can you imagine how he'd feel about being in a sailing race?"

"He'd be in heaven," said Claud.

"The only thing," I went on, "is that he'd probably rather go in your boat than in mine." (Claudia and Jamie are very close.) "Do you think the girls would mind splitting up? Either Becca or Haley would have to go with you and Jamie, and the other one could come with Jeff and me. I'm positive Jeff will want to be in my boat. We'd still be quite well balanced in terms of our crew members."

"Listen, before we get carried away with details," said Claud, "we'd better ring the Braddocks and the Newtons and get their

27

permission. For all we know, they might be going away this weekend."

But they weren't. The adults were delighted with the invitations for Haley and Jamie, as long as we promised to follow all the safety rules, like making them wear life jackets. We promised.

And on Wednesday, I had another idea for our race. "Claud," I said to her in the school cafeteria that day, "instead of just racing to Greenpoint and back, how about making this a real outing for Jeff and the children?"

"What kind of outing?" asked Claud.

"Well, we could race just *to* Greenpoint, not to Greenpoint and back. We could pack picnic lunches, and after the race, we could stay on the island for an hour or two, eat, let the children play in the water and look for shells and things, and then we could have a leisurely sail back home. That way, we'd still get our race, and the children could have some fun too."

"I think that's a great idea!" exclaimed Claud. "We'll just have to get the parents' permission, that's all."

We took care of everything that afternoon. We talked to the Newtons and to my mum, to the Braddocks and to Jessi. Her parents weren't at home, but she was sure they'd agree to the outing since they'd already agreed to the race. Becca and Haley even said they wouldn't mind going in different boats.

We were all set to sail!

4th CHAPTER

Dawn

Looking Back-Friday

I think that if I hadn't been so determined to win the race, I would never have had the fight with Mary Anne, and then what happened on the island wouldn't have seemed quite so bad. But we did have a fight and it was basically my fault. I say basically because, as Mary Anne's father always points out, "It takes two to tango". By that he means you can't have a one-sided fight. Mary Anne — and Logan — were part of the problem, too. But when you get right down to it, it was my fault....

29

Up, down. Up, down. Up, down. Puff, puff, puff, puff.

I was lying on a towel in the lounge working out to one of those exercise videos. The woman on the video seemed to have boundless energy, and I was proud to say that I did, too.

It was Friday afternoon, the day before the replay. I'd been working out all week. And I'd been filling up on healthy, high-energy food. Of course, I didn't tell Claudia that. I was pretty sure she was sticking to her junk-food diet and not exercising at all. She rarely does. Exercise, that is.

"All right!" said the video woman brightly. She bounced to her feet from a sitting position. How did she do that? Every time I reached that point in the tape I fell over. When I got up I had to stop the tape, rewind it, and start at the place where I'd keeled over sideways and fallen behind the instructions.

"And *one*, and *two*, and *three*, and *four*," said the instructor. "*Lift* those legs. *Lift* those legs. Higher! Higher! *You* can *do* it!"

She sounded rather silly, but the funny thing was, I found that if I tried, I *could* do it. I lifted my legs higher than the day before.

The video woman started running on the spot. I ran with her. We were running to the song "Give My Regards to Broadway", which made us run pretty fast. I have to admit, I was relieved when the phone rang. I was the only one at home, so I would have to put the tape on "pause" to answer it.

Click. The video woman froze in mid-run.

"I'll be right back," I told her.

I grabbed a small towel from the arm of a chair and patted myself dry as I made a dash for the phone. I was all sweaty and out of breath.

"Hello?" I said, panting, as I picked up the receiver.

"Dawn? Is that you?" It was Logan Bruno, Mary Anne's boyfriend.

"Yes," I gasped.

"What were you doing?"

"Exercising." Pant, pant, pant.

"Oh. Sorry. Listen, is Mary Anne there?"

"No, she's sitting at the Perkinses' for a little while."

"Okay. Well, I've got a problem. Mary Anne and I were supposed to meet at the library at about four-thirty—as soon as she finished at the Perkinses', I suppose. But Hunter's just had an asthma attack and Mum's taken him to the doctor, so I've got to stay here with Kerry until they get back, and I don't know when that'll be."

Logan's little brother, Hunter, is allergic to everything in the world, and sometimes gets asthma attacks, which can be frightening. Kerry is Logan's younger sister. It was lucky that Logan was at home to look after her.

"Gosh! I'm really sorry, Logan. I'll ring Mary

31

Anne at the Perkinses' for you and tell her what's happened. I hope Hunter's okay."

"Thanks, Dawn."

We rang off and I was about to call Mary Anne when the phone rang again. This time it was Mum.

"Hello, dear!" she said. "I'm just calling to tell you that I spoke to Richard a few minutes ago and we've decided to go out for an early dinner tonight. We thought it would be a nice way to start the weekend."

"Oh, great, Mum. Have fun!"

"Thanks. You and Mary Anne will be okay, won't you? If you don't see anything in the fridge you like, then go ahead and get a takeaway Chinese or something."

"All right! Thanks!" I wasn't sure if Chinese food was healthy, filling stuff, but it sounded good. I was looking around the kitchen for our Chinese menus when I heard the video go on in the lounge. The "pause" was over. I ran to the lounge, began the workout again, and had got as far as two running steps when the phone rang for a third time.

"Bother!" I exclaimed. I put the tape on "pause" and dashed back to the kitchen.

"Hello?" I said, picking up the phone.

"Hi, Sunshine! It's your old dad."

"Hi, Old Dad!"

"I just wanted to let you know that Jeff's safely on his way."

"Okay. We'll pick up him late tonight. Mum and Richard are going out to dinner, but we'll all be at the airport in plenty of time to meet Jeff. I can't wait to see him."

"Well, have a nice weekend. Jeff told me about the race. Good luck! I know you'll win."

When Dad and I finished on the phone, I hung around in the kitchen, waiting for the phone to ring again. When it didn't I *finally* returned to my workout and was able to keep at it without interruptions. I decided to exercise until almost five o'clock (if I could stand it), then quickly shower and change my clothes. That would give me just enough time to get to the Friday BSC meeting.

"And *one*, and *two* . . ."

I managed to exercise until 4:45. Then I had to stop. My muscles felt as if they were coiled springs—too tight. I cooled down for a while, went upstairs, peeled off my sweaty workout clothes, and stepped into the shower.

Ahhhh! I stood there for ever, just letting the hot water spray on my back. At last I had to turn off the water, though. If I didn't, I wouldn't be dry and dressed in time for the meeting.

It was just as I slipping a shirt over my head that I heard our front door open and then close with a bang.

"Mary Anne?" I called. "Is that you?"

"Yes," she answered shortly. She sounded pretty cross.

The next sound I heard was footsteps pounding up the stairs and into Mum and Richard's room.

"Hey!" I said. "Is something the matter?"

"Yes, something *is* the matter. Logan stood me up, that's what."

By that time I was leaning against the doorway to our parents' room. Mary Anne was sitting in a chair, dialling Logan's number on the phone.

Uh-oh! I thought. I didn't ring the Perkinses' to give Logan's message to Mary Anne.

"Um, Mary Anne," I began.

But Mary Anne was already saying, "Logan?" and waving her hand at me to be quiet.

From then on I could only hear Mary Anne's end of the conversation, of course, but from the things she said I had a pretty good idea what was going on. And I've hardly ever seen Mary Anne so angry.

"Logan! What are you doing at home? Have you been there all afternoon? We were supposed to meet at the library at four-thirty. Where were you? You stood me up!"

Logan must have said something like, "I didn't stand you up," because Mary Anne said, "Well, you weren't there. I waited and waited."

"Mary *Anne*!" I hissed.

Mary Anne put her hand over the receiver and

34

said, "SHHH! Logan and I are *trying* to have an argument. Would you please leave me alone?"

I stopped leaning against the doorway and edged out into the hallway where I could hear the rest of the coversation. I knew Logan and Mary Anne would work out what I'd done and that I'd be in trouble pretty soon. I wanted to be prepared for it.

The next thing I heard Mary Anne say was, "How could you stand me up? Did you just forget? Or did you have something better to do?"

Logan must have said he had something better to do and then told her about Hunter's asthma attack and his call to me. Because soon Mary Anne was saying, "Well, Dawn never called me," and "Logan, I'm so sorry."

But apparently Logan wasn't accepting Mary Anne's apology. I suppose he just couldn't believe that Mary Anne would think he'd stand her up. Mary Anne kept saying, "I'm sor—Logan, I'm really—Logan, I'm sorry. I—" But Logan wouldn't let her get a word in edgeways. Which of course made Mary Anne crosser than ever with him.

Finally, she slammed the phone down on him!

Whoops! I thought, as I fled to my room. (I didn't want Mary Anne to know I'd been eavesdropping.) When Mary Anne appeared at the door to my room (which took all of about two seconds), she just stood there and glared at me.

Before she could say a word, I blurted out, "I'm sorry, I'm sorry, I'm sorry. Logan gave me the message for you and I was going to ring you right away, but before I could, Mum rang, and then Dad rang, and I suppose—I, I just forgot . . . I *meant* to tell you."

"But you didn't."

I changed the subject. "I've never heard you put the phone down on Logan before."

"Were you *eaves*dropping?" Mary Anne's voice was growing shrill.

I looked at my watch. "Uh-oh! If we don't hurry we're going to be late for the meeting." I took off down the stairs.

Mary Anne followed, but she didn't stop arguing. We argued all the time we were riding our bicycles over to Claud's house, the BSC headquarters.

"Didn't you *tell* Logan I forgot to give you the message?" I asked as we pedalled towards Bradford Court.

"Of course I did," she snapped. "But he's angry with me for thinking he'd stand me up."

I sighed. Logan and Mary Anne usually understand each other so well. This fight was unlike them. So I felt terrible. Because of me, Logan and Mary Anne were *very* angry with each other. And Mary Anne was furious with me. So furious, in fact, that as we parked our bikes on the Kishis' driveway, she said, "You know what? I

36

wish I never had to see you again. I wish you would get out of my life—for ever."

5th
CHAPTER

Claudia

Looking Back —
Satruday mornig and afternon

Uh oh! Dawn and mary Ann aren't speaking to each other. I felt sorry for Dawn, on the other hand mabe if she cant corkin cjks keeps her mind on the race Ill win but then it woldnt realy be fiar.

I tired not to think of my friends figt. I tired to think of the race and the picknick insted. I packed a baskit full of food I tired to pack stuff that wold be helthy for the kids but I couldnt help paking a lot of chocolate ta.

Saturday was another perfect day for sailing. I woke up to a clear blue sky with some puffy white clouds and just enough breeze to make our sailing race fun and challenging.

That morning I dressed sensibly for our replay. No jewellery at all (I wasn't going to lose because of my earrings) and a long-sleeved top I could tuck into my jeans. I even pulled my hair back and plaited it so it wouldn't blow in my face.

At about ten o'clock my phone rang. I was just finishing putting on my make-up. (I didn't see how I could possibly lose a race because of *make-up*.) I put the lid back on my mascara and picked up the receiver.

"Hello?" I said. (Sometimes I forget and say, "Hello, Babysitters Club," even when we aren't having a meeting.)

"Hi, it's me." Dawn. My friends and I know each other so well, we don't even have to say who's calling.

"Are you chickening out?" I asked immediately.

"No!"

"Oh. What's the matter?"

"I was calling to see if you were chickening out."

"No! I'm ready to go. I'm going to beat you hollow."

"We'll see."

"Are you and Mary Anne speaking to each other?" I asked.

There was a pause. Finally Dawn said, "Not exactly." Then she changed her mind and said, "Not at all."

I wasn't sure how to respond to that. Luckily, Dawn didn't seem to need a response. She went on talking. "What, um, what are you wearing?" she asked. I could tell she was trying not to laugh.

"Jeans, a polo-neck, trainers, and a visor. And my hair's plaited, and I haven't got any jewellery on," I answered indignantly.

"I'm just teasing you," Dawn said. "Listen, I've packed muesli bars, sugar-free peanut butter sandwiches, bananas, some salad made without mayonnaise—you know, so it won't go bad—some yoghurt, a few cartons of orange juice, and a lot of bottled spring water for Jeff and me. We love spring water. What are you putting in your picnic basket?" she asked.

"Salami sandwiches, apples, a big bottle of Coke, and fifteen bars of chocolate. Do you think we've got enough food?"

"Enough for an army," said Dawn. "Okay. I'll see you at the community centre at eleven o'clock. Be there or be be square."

I giggled. Then we rang off.

An hour later, a crowd of people was at the quayside. There were my parents, my sister, and me; Dawn, her mother, and her stepfather; Jessi, Becca, and Squirt (who'd been driven over by

Haley and her family, who were also there); Jamie, his parents, and his baby sister; Kristy; Stacey; Mallory, her father, and two of her brothers, who were all going to go sailing themselves later; and a few helpers.

Mary Anne and Logan weren't there. That was because Logan was angry with Mary Anne, and Mary Anne was angry with Dawn.

Dawn and I had each chosen a boat for the race. We'd put our picnic baskets into them, made sure each boat had a first-aid kit and three life jackets, and now we were coating ourselves and the children with suntan oil.

While this was going on—in fact, while I was rubbing sun oil on every part of Jamie's body that wasn't covered up—he and his mother were having this conversation:

"Darling, I don't know if you should really go."

"But I feel fine, Mummy."

"But you had the sniffles yesterday."

"I *still* feel fine."

"I don't know . . ."

"*Please*? Please, please, *please*? I promise I'll never quarrel with Lucy again." (Lucy is Jamie's sister.) "And I'll do whatever you tell me from now on. I'll tidy my room, and I won't leave my trainers on the stairs—"

"Okay, okay, okay." Mrs Newton gave in. Almost. "Are you *sure* you feel okay?"

41

"I . . . FEEL . . . *FINE*!"

"OKAY!"

Jamie and his mother were laughing by then.

I jumped into the conversation. "I promise I'll make Jamie wear his windcheater all day," I told Mrs Newton. "Then he won't get cold. And he'll have to wear shoes on the boat, so don't worry about cold feet. And if anything seems wrong, we'll just turn round and come back, okay?"

Mrs Newton smiled. "All right. I suppose I'm just a bit nervous. The last time Jamie had the sniffles, it turned into pneumonia."

Pneumonia? Anyway, Jamie looked fine to me. He wasn't even sniffling.

"Okay!" shouted Dawn from behind me. "Who's ready to go sailing?"

"I am!" cried Jamie, Jeff, Haley, and Becca.

The children followed us to our boats. Dawn and I strapped life jackets onto the children. Then we strapped life jackets onto ourselves. We always wear them. Anything could happen, and hey presto! you'd find yourself in the water. Even the best swimmer needs to be prepared.

When the children were ready, Dawn suddenly became very official.

"Life jackets?" she asked.

"Check," I replied, without bothering to look, since we'd *just* strapped everybody in and the helpers had helped us.

"Food?"

"Check."

"First-aid kits?"

"Check."

"Let's go!"

Then Jamie, Haley, and Becca turned nervous on us. They ran back to their families for extra hugs. For just a moment, I thought the Newtons were going to talk Jamie into staying at home. But they didn't. A few minutes later, Jamie, Becca, and I were settled in one boat, and Dawn, Jeff, and Haley were in another.

A helper was poised on the quay. "Ready!" he shouted. "Get set, . . . GO!"

He lowered his arm as though he was starting a car race.

I almost giggled, but I knew I had to concentrate on the replay.

We were off. Behind us I could hear people calling things like, "Goodbye!" and, "Have fun!" and, "See you later!" and, "Wear your wind-cheater!" (Guess who said that.)

As we sailed along, we picked up speed. I love the feeling of wind. I think that's why I like to ski, too. I was glad I'd tied my hair back, though.

I started to concentrate. We could see Green-point Island, so we knew where we were going. I felt strong. I felt powerful.

"Claudia?" said Becca after a bit.

"What?" I replied.

"This is so wonderful!" I could hardly hear

43

Becca, but it wasn't just because of the wind rushing by. She was speaking quietly, as though she was in a church or something. And I knew why. We were out on the water, away from the edge of our country. If we just kept going and going we would hit . . . I wasn't sure what. I used to think it was England, but Janine the Genius told me I was wrong. Anyway, there was nothing but air above us and water below us. And land, but that was far off in the distance. It was, as Becca had said, wonderful.

For a while, my boat was ahead. Although I listened to Becca, and kept a careful eye on her and Jamie, I was doing my best sailing.

"Hey, you lot!" yelled Jamie to Dawn's boat, which wasn't far behind. "We're going to win this race. We're going to beat you."

I wasn't sure whether Dawn and Jeff and Haley could hear Jamie until Haley yelled back, "You're not!"

"We are too!" said Becca.

"You're not!"

"We *are!*"

After a while, Dawn's boat caught up with ours. She grinned at me. I gritted my teeth. The shouting went on till Dawn pulled ahead.

And that was how we spent the next hour or so. First one boat was ahead, then another. The children kept on yelling things to each other and giggling. Jamie claimed he was starving, so he ate

44

a peanut butter sandwich. Then Becca said *she* was starving and ate an apple and a chocolate bar.

"Hey, save some room and some food for the pic—"I started to say.

But I was interrupted by a shout from Dawn. "Claudia, look!" she cried. She was pointing to the sky.

I looked up. Huge thunderclouds were forming. A chill ran through my body, even though the sun was still shining brightly. A storm was brewing, and Dawn and I both knew that out here—on this beautiful water—a storm could become a squall and sneak up on you quickly.

And be really nasty.

"Dawn!" I yelled, our race already forgotten. "We'd better decide what to do—and fast!"

6th CHAPTER

Dawn

Looking back —
Saturday afternoon
Claud and I knew we were
in trouble the second we saw
those clouds. Well, I knew,
anyway, and I'm pretty sure
from the look on Claud's face
that she knew, too. I think even
Jeff did. But Becca, Haley, and
Jamie didn't look nervous until
the storm actually hit us. And I
have to give them credit for this.
All three of them kept their
heads, especially the girls.
Jamie cried, but what else
would you expect from a four-
year-old? I tried hard not to
think about lost boats and
shipwrecks....

The clouds piled up until they looked like mountains in the sky, and a haze formed quickly. None of this took as long as you might think. In fact, it happened more quickly than Claud or I would have expected. Soon, I knew, the sky would be a mass of dark clouds.

I steered my boat as close to Claudia's as I could, which wasn't easy, considering the wind that was blowing up.

"Claud!" I shouted. I had to yell loudly in order for her to hear me.

"Yes?"

"We'd better turn back."

"No!" Claudia shook her head. "I know we can't see it any more, but we're closer to Greenpoint now than we are to the shore. If we keep going ahead, we might reach the island. If we turn round, we probably won't . . . you know." Claudia glanced at Jamie and Becca. She was trying not to scare them.

Even though Claudia had grown up here and knew Greenpoint and this area much better than I did, I shouted back to her, "Are you *sure* we shouldn't turn round?"

"Positive!"

So we kept moving ahead. Sailing was becoming a struggle. I told Jeff what we were up against because I knew he could cope with it, and would then be a help. He tightened the straps on our life jackets and made Haley sit down out of the way.

47

Then he secured anything that might blow away.

Claudia didn't have such help. She was on her own in her boat, holding the sail, trying to steer, checking life jackets, doing everything herself.

As the wind blew even harder and the first drops of rain began to fall, I noticed that Claudia's boat was ahead of mine.

"Hurray!" yelled Jamie, obviously unaware of trouble.

But I yelled, "Claud, let the sail out—we must stay together! We can't let ourselves get separated."

"I'm trying to stay with you," she called back, and I could barely hear her. "But the wind's awfully strong."

So were the waves. The water was growing choppier by the second. Our boat was being tossed so fiercely by the sea that sometimes a wave would slap right over it. At other times we were bounced up into the air.

"It's just like a water ride at the amusement park!" said Haley gleefully as Jeff rushed around, covering things with plastic sheets. I was extremely glad he was there.

By that time, the sky had grown so dark that it looked almost like night. I could barely see Claud's boat.

"Claudia?" I shouted.

"Don't worry. I'm here!"

Okay. She was over to our right.

48

And then, without warning, that black, black sky just opened up. It was as if it were so full of rain that it couldn't hold it in any longer. And the only thing it could do was dump all the water on us.

Which it did.

The rain came down in sheets. Now Jeff tried to cover himself and Haley and me with the plastic, but it didn't do any good. The wind blew it off us, and the plastic was whisked away into the darkness.

"Dawn? Dawn?" Claudia was calling to me.

"I'm here. I'm still to your left!" I yelled.

If only we could see each other, I thought. And then I *could* see Claud—but just her face. It was lit up against the storm.

"Your torch!" she called. "You've got a torch under the seat next to the first-aid kit."

Jeff found it and switched it on. It didn't light our way (it wasn't strong enough), but at least Claud and I could keep track of each other.

It was at this point, with the choppy water, the sheets of rain, and the gusty wind, that Haley said to me, "Dawn? I don't want to be rude or anything, but I'm not having fun any more."

"Well, we're in a little trouble," I told Haley. "This is a bad storm. We're trying to reach Greenpoint Island but I'm not sure we're on course. The best thing to do is just hold on tight. And if I give you any instructions, follow them. No questions asked, okay?"

49

"Okay," replied Haley shakily.

In Claud's boat, Becca grew nervous faster than Haley did, and Jamie began to cry. He cried hard at first, but soon he was just sniffling. Everybody held together as best they could.

And then it happened.

A *huge* wave washed over our boat. Haley was thrown off her seat by the force of it. Remembering my instructions to "hold on tight," she grabbed for the nearest object—which happened to be the rudder. The rudder snapped and Haley went flying again. This time *I* made a grab for her. I caught her life jacket.

Haley was safe.

But from the other end of the boat Jeff was screaming, "Dawn! The boat's full of water!"

"Well, that was a big wave," I pointed out.

"No, it's not just that. There's water coming in from somewhere else!" Jeff was frantically trying to rescue our supplies while I settled Haley on a seat again. I noticed that she was in water halfway up to her knees. Whoa! This was serious.

"Hey! You lot!" yelled Claudia. "Stay with us! You keep drifting away!"

"Our rudder's broken!" I shouted. "And our boat's filling up with water!"

It was at that point, as I noticed Claudia's torch bobbing away, that Jeff, trying not to sound frightened, crossed the boat and tried to whisper to me (which was not easy), "We're sinking."

"We're what!" I'd heard him, but I didn't want to believe him.

"We're sinking," he repeated quietly.

I looked at Haley. The water was creeping closer to her knees.

"I think we're going to have to bail out," I told him. "We'll try to get Claud to steer as close to us as she can—"

"Then I'll throw our supplies to her," Jeff interrupted.

"Oh, good thinking," I said, "and then we'll have to . . . just hold on to her boat and float, I suppose. We can't get into the boat. We'll be too heavy. I'll help you and Haley, since I've passed my life-saving test."

"Okay." No arguments from Jeff.

"Claud!" I yelled again.

"What?"

"We're going to have to bail out and swim to your boat. There's nothing else to do. We're sinking."

"Okay," replied Claud tightly. I could tell she was nervous. Six people and one small sailing boat wasn't a good idea. There would be too much weight. But what choice did we have?

"Can you steer over here?" I yelled. My teeth were chattering. The sea and the rain were cold.

"I'll try."

The torch on Claud's boat bobbed closer to ours. Soon I could actually make out Claudia,

51

Jamie, and Becca. They looked terrified—and as cold as I felt.

"First," I yelled to Claud, "Jeff's going to throw our supplies to you. We'd better hang on to everything we can."

"Okay!" Claud replied, and she and Becca caught the things as Jeff threw them. They tried to pack them away under the seats or in plastic.

"All right, now we're going to swim to your boat," I said, trying to stay calm. At that point, it didn't look difficult. Claudia was right next to us. I thought we could reach her without much swimming—but immediately a huge wave separated us.

"Okay, you first, Haley," I said, climbing overboard. "I'll help you."

"I don't *want* to go in the water!" she cried.

"I'm sorry, but you have to. I'll swim you to Claudia and she and Becca will help you hang on to their boat. There's no room for us *in* the boat. Remember, you've got your life jacket on, so you can't sink."

Haley looked at our boat. She saw that water was filling it rapidly.

"Okay, here goes," she said bravely. She held her nose (which was unnecessary because of the life jacket) and jumped overboard. Just in time I found her hand and swam with her. I didn't want us separated.

The distance to Claudia's boat wasn't too far,

thankfully, and Haley doggy paddled to it fairly quickly, with just a little help from me. Claudia and Becca pulled her to the side, and Becca grabbed her wrists.

Then I turned round and went back for Jeff. He was poised to jump in—and leave our boat behind.

"Go ahead!" I yelled to Jeff.

Splash! I caught Jeff as he jumped in. Then, hand-in-hand, we swam to Claudia's boat. He and I clung to the sides without help. We were on our own.

"Claud?" I shouted. "Are we still on course?"

"I've no idea," she replied. "It's been so windy. But—Hey, wait! I can see land ahead! Maybe it's Greenpoint!"

"Hurray!" cheered Jamie, through chattering teeth.

In just a few minutes, I could feel sand under my feet. We really had reached land. We dragged the boat ashore and unloaded the supplies. The rain was easing up. The sky was brightening.

"Come on, you lot, we've got to find shelter and dry out," said Claud, taking charge.

I was glad to let her do so. I didn't feel up to it.

So Jeff, Haley, and Becca began unloading our things from the boat. While they were busy, Claudia turned to me. "You know what?" she said.

Dawn

"What?" I replied.

"This isn't Greenpoint Island. I don't know where we are."

I felt like crying.

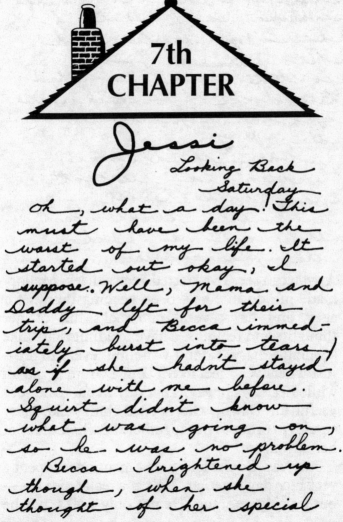

7th CHAPTER

Jessi

Looking Back
Saturday

Oh —, what a day! This
must have been the
worst of my life. It
started out okay, I
suppose. Well, Mama and
Daddy left for their
trip, and Becca immed-
iately burst into tears,
as if she hadn't stayed
alone with me before.
Squirt didn't know
what was going on,
so he was no problem.
Becca brightened up
though, when she
thought of her special

*sailing trip. And
by the time she'd
put on her swimming
costume, a T-shirt, a
pair of shorts, and
her trainers, she
couldn't wait for the
Braddocks to pick us
up and take us to
the quay.*

*Once she'd gone,
I spent a pleasant
day with Squirt —
until the thunderstorm.
That put an end to
the pleasantness....*

As you can see, I've started keep a diary. Mallory made me do it. She's been keeping diaries for ages, and has several notebooks full of her thoughts and feelings. I have to admit that I like keeping a diary. I don't write in it every night—just whenever I feel like it. But I wrote in it a lot while Becca was away. That turned out to be very useful for Dawn, who needed things like diary entries in order to put together the whole story of her adventure.

Anyway, Squirt and I, as I mentioned, spent a very nice day together. He's at a really nice age—but a tiring one, too. He not only walks, but he runs (sort of) and he's still a fast crawler. By the time he went upstairs for his afternoon nap on Saturday, I was exhausted. (How does my mother do it, all day, every day?) I was hoping to make myself a nice glass of iced tea, put my feet up, and lose myself in *Stormy, Misty's Foal*, which I've read only about a million times. But I'd only read two pages when—*BAM*!

Thunder.

Squirt was awake instantly. That was the end of his nap and my nice rest period.

Squirt hates thunder. He kept putting his hands over his ears and crying big alligator tears.

"Shh, shh," I said softly. "It'll be over soon. And then Becca will come back and we'll have hot dogs for dinner. How about that?"

Well, things didn't go exactly as I'd planned. In fact, they went as far as possible in the other direction.

At five o'clock (the thunderstorm over), I said brightly to Squirt, "Becca will be home any minute now!"

At five-thirty, I said to him, "I wonder where your sister is? I'm getting hungry for hot dogs and I bet you are, too."

At six, I said, sounding really worried, "Where on earth is Becca? She should be home by now. If she's playing at Haley's and didn't tell me, she's in trouble."

I rang the Braddocks.

Jessi

"Hi, Mr Braddock," I began. And just as I said, "Is Becca at your house playing with Haley?" *he* said, "Is Haley at your house playing with Becca?"

Then we both said, "No," at the same time.

"I don't think they're back yet," said Mr Braddock, and I knew he meant Claudia, Dawn, and their sailing crews.

"But they should be back by now!" I cried.

I wanted to believe that they really were back, so I rang Mary Anne next. "Dawn's back, isn't she?" I asked her nervously.

"I don't know and I don't care," replied Mary Anne haughtily.

"Come on," I said. "This is important. Is she back?"

"No," said Mary Anne.

I rang the Kishis and the Newtons next, knowing very well that they would say Claudia and Jamie weren't back, either.

I was right.

At long last I did what I'd been dreading. I rang the community centre. A very nice woman answered the phone. When I told her who I was and why I was calling, she started to sound worried. "Mr Braddock and several other parents have phoned during the last half hour," she told me. "We haven't seen the boats. And they should have been back by now. I think it's time to take some action."

58

Jessi

"Um," I began, fear welling up inside me, "do you think they got caught in that storm we had here a while ago?"

"That's hard to say," the woman replied. "It depends on where it came from. If they *did* get caught in it, let's just hope they were already on Greenpoint."

"What kind of action are you going to take?" I asked.

"We'll call the Coastguard and send out some search boats—I think. It's going to be dark soon, and it's starting to rain again. Those aren't ideal searching conditions. Do you want to come to the centre and help us?"

I did, but I had to say, "I'm really sorry, but I can't. My parents are away for the weekend. I've got to stay here and look after my baby brother."

"Okay," replied the woman. "Give me your phone number and we'll keep you posted."

"Thanks," I said. As I rang off it suddenly dawned on me: this was an emergency. My parents had left a long list of emergency numbers for the weekend. Most of them didn't apply—like the numbers for our doctor and the ambulance and the fire brigade. But I thought I ought to call Dr Johanssen. The Johanssens are our neighbours and Becca is best friends with their daughter, Charlotte. Perhaps they could look after Squirt for me so that I could go to the centre and help?

I dialled the Johanssens' number. No answer.

Jessi

I wanted to ring the Pikes next—they'd be good in an emergency—but next on Mum's list of names and numbers was (gulp) my dreaded Aunt Cecelia. Aunt Cecelia is Daddy's older sister.

I can't stand her.

She wears smelly perfume and always looks as if she's just been eating a lemon. Her lips are permanently pursed. She disapproves of everything and treats Becca and me like absolute infants. Aunt Cecelia used to live in New Jersey with the rest of our relatives, but recently her husband died and she decided she couldn't live in their house any more so she moved to Queenstown, Connecticut, which is much too close for my liking.

If I rang her and told her what was going on, I had a feeling she'd be over in a flash.

I must have ESP. I was right about everything. In no time at all Aunt Cecelia zoomed up our driveway in her old Volkswagen, barged through the front door, and began saying (through pursed lips), "How could a couple of intelligent adults leave an eleven-year-old in charge of two younger children for three whole days? And how could you *and* your parents be irresponsible enough to let Rebecca go out in a sailing boat?"

"It wasn't my fau—" I started to say, but Aunt Cecelia was already on the phone.

First she rang the community centre. "No

60

Jessi

news," she said curtly as she hung up. "I'll have
to ring your parents."

"My parents!" I exclaimed. "No! You'll ruin
their holi—"

"This is a serious matter, Jessica. It worries me
that you don't understand that. Who knows what
has happened to your sister? Your parents must
be told what is going on."

Luckily, my parents weren't in their hotel
room, so Aunt Cecelia just left a message for them
to ring back.

As soon as my aunt rang off, the phone rang. I
grabbed for it and got it before she did. (I think I
took her by surprise.) I knew I was being rude,
but I didn't care.

The caller was Mallory.

"Thank goodness it's you!" I exclaimed.

"Listen," said Mal, without asking why I
sounded so relieved, "I want you to know that *we*
know what's happened. Mum and Dad and my
brothers and even Vanessa are helping to search.
Nothing's turned up yet. I thought you might like
some company, though, so I arranged for Margo
and Claire to go and stay with Stacey's mum and
I'm coming to your house. Right now. Okay?"

I was delighted, but I felt it was only fair to
warn Mal about Aunt Cecelia. Mallory said she
didn't care, and proceeded to ride her bike over
here in the rain. I was especially grateful for her
company. Aunt Cecelia had taken complete charge

61

Jessi

of Squirt, dinner, and everything else. Without Mal, there would be nothing for me to do but worry.

Mal and I sat by the phone. At eight o'clock it rang. We jumped a mile. But it was only Kristy on the other end, saying that she was calling an emergency meeting of what was left of the BSC for the next morning—if no progress had been made in the search for the missing boaters.

8th CHAPTER

Dawn

Looking Back-
Saturday evening

Claudia and I knew we weren't on Greenpoint Island, but we weren't sure whether to tell the others. That was just a tiny dilemma, though. We had many more important matters on our minds as we stood, dripping and shivering, on the shore of the island. Like... what to do next. Find shelter? All I wanted to do was get dry, but I couldn't think how. Everything was wet. I was grateful to let Claudia take over.

The first problem that we managed to solve was the smallest one, and it was solved by accident. Haley, who had been to Greenpoint several times with her family, looked around as the sky continued to brighten, and said, "You know something? We're on the wrong island!"

"What do you mean?" asked Jeff, glancing at me suspiciously.

"Well, um, she's right," I managed to say. "We blew off course."

"How much off course?" asked Jeff.

I looked at Claud. She shrugged. Then she said, "It doesn't matter. It won't help us to know. Come on, all of you. First order of business" (she sounded like Kristy) "is to find some sort of shelter. Then we'll build a fire and dry out and get nice and warm."

"Goody!" said Haley, and then she began to sing, "*We're off to find a shelter!*" She sang it to the tune of "We're Off to See the Wizard" from the film *The Wizard of Oz*.

"*A wonderful shelter we'll find,*" added Haley.

Jeff and I loaded all the supplies from the boat into our arms, handing a few to Haley and Becca, and Claudia picked up the shivering Jamie.

We looked around. Where exactly were we going? The island had a nice beach. And the inland part looked dark and green, like a forest. I wondered how big the island was.

"Let's head for the trees," said Claudia.

64

Haley wanted to continue the song. *"We're off to find a shelter! A wonderful shelter we'll find. We hear there is a wonderful place, a wonderful, wonderful place. If ever a, ever a shelter there was, this island . . . um . . . this island . . ."*

That was as far as she got with her song. Becca didn't help her. She's too shy to sing in front of a lot of people.

We headed into the trees but immediately came out again. The ground was drier in there, but the trees dripped on us and we didn't like the darkness at all. So we wandered along at the edge of the trees. All I could see behind me and in front of me were trees and beach.

"Is this a *desert* island?" asked Haley, wide-eyed.

"I hope not," replied Claudia. "If it is, we're *way* off course. There aren't any desert islands off the coast of Connecticut."

"Deserted ones," I added, "but not actual desert islands."

"Gosh, well, anyway this is a bit like a book I read called *Baby Island*." Haley began to tell us all about it.

That was when Jeff told us about *The Cay*.

And *that* was when Becca stopped in her tracks and said, "Hey, what's that? That hole over there?"

"That hole" turned out to be a cave. We'd come to a huge pile of boulders. That was the only

65

way to describe them. They were the biggest rocks I'd ever seen. Great slabs of something (granite, maybe) all piled on top of each other. And three of them had formed a gigantic triangular space. It was high enough to walk into without bending over, and definitely wide enough and deep enough for six people.

Jeff and I put our supplies down on the sand and turned on the torches.

"I suppose we ought to check this out, hadn't we?" I said to Claudia nervously. I was afraid of what we might find in the cave.

"Yes," she said, looking at the sky, which was now growing dark again, and not just because evening was approaching. The sky was dark with clouds.

Jeff and I approached the cave cautiously. I glanced back once at Claudia, and she said, "Do you want me to go instead, Dawn?" I did— badly—but Jamie had laid his head on her shoulder and looked miserable, so I just said, "That's okay."

Jeff and I went into the cave. We shone our torches around as if we were expecting to find pirates guarding their treasure. Instead we found —nothing! Just the space between the boulders. And it was warm and dry.

"Hey, Claud! Come here!" I shouted.

Claudia, holding Jamie, ran up to us, followed by Becca and Haley. They peered curiously inside, watching as Jeff and I shone our torches into every nook and cranny.

"Do you think it's safe?" I asked Claudia.

She nodded. "These rocks have probably been here for ever. I bet they're more solid than our houses at home."

So we unpacked our supplies, and then Jeff, Becca, and Haley looked around in the woods (but not too far away) for some dry sticks and leaves so that we could start a fire. This wasn't easy, considering all the rain, and they were gone for quite a while.

"I'm hungry," whined Jamie, so Claudia found him a still-dry peanut butter sandwich. (Thank goodness for clingfilm.)

While he was eating it, Claud and I held a whispered conversation at the other end of the cave.

"What are we going to do now?" I asked.

"Well, the boat's still in good condition," Claud replied.

"Yes, but there's only one boat and there are six of us."

"I know. I was thinking that tomorrow, or whenever the weather clears, you and Jeff, or maybe Jeff and I, could take the boat, sail back to shore, and send the Coastguard out here to rescue the others."

"Oh, Claud. I don't know. I mean, we don't know how far out we are, or if we can see the shore

67

from here. And since we've walked part-way around the island, we don't know which direction the shore is in. Whoever goes out in that boat could easily get lost at sea." I was nearly in tears. All I could really think about were the last words Mary Anne had spoken to me: "I wish I never had to see you again. I wish you would get out of my life—for ever." Well . . . maybe I would.

Claudia put her arm round me. Then she whispered, "I know you're scared. I'm scared, too. But we don't want to frighten the children." (She glanced over her shoulder at Jamie.) "So let's just pretend everything's okay. We'll talk about this later."

It began to rain again then, and just as I went to the cave entrance to call Jeff and the girls, they appeared, grinning broadly. Their arms were full of dry sticks, twigs, and leaves.

"We found them under this big rock that was sticking out," announced Haley proudly. "*Every-thing* under it was dry!"

The children piled their findings in the middle of the cave. Then we looked at each other. The same thought had occurred to all of us.

"How are we going to light it?" asked Becca.

"Rubbing two sticks together could take all night," added Jeff.

"I suppose nobody's got any matches," I said unnecessarily.

For some reason, Jeff brightened at that.

"What? You've got *matches* on you?" I asked.

"No. But I bet there are some in the survival kit I found when you and I were taking all the stuff out of Claudia's boat."

We made a dash for our things. Sure enough, there was a survival kit, containing exactly seven matches—and not much else. ("I'll have to speak to the people at the centre about this," muttered Claudia.) But at least we got a fire going.

"Okay. Everyone dry out," I ordered.

We sat round the fire until we felt more comfortable.

"Now we'd better see about our food," said Claud. "Just in case we're here for a while, we've got to see how much of it can be saved, and then we'd better ration it—you know, eat a little at a time to make it last as long as possible." Jeff hauled the picnic baskets nearer to the fire, where we could see better. The baskets were soaked, of course, but he opened them up and found that they weren't in bad shape. The bottles of water, the big bottle of Coke, and the cartons of orange juice were fine, of course. Warm, but fine. We put them in the coolest spot we could find in the cave. The muesli bars were soaked and had to be thrown away. The sandwiches in their cling film were okay, but we decided to eat all of them for dinner, since we didn't know how long sugar-free peanut butter and (ugh!) salami would last without a fridge. We decided to eat the salad for the same reason, and the yoghurt, too, but we saved the bananas, apples and chocolate.

"What if we ate all this food and had to start eating clams?" said Becca.

"Or insects and worms?" said Haley, giggling.

"Snakes!" shrieked Jamie, and we laughed nervously.

Then Jeff said, "You know what? That Coke has been tossed around all day. Imagine what would happen if we opened it now!"

Nobody could stop laughing.

Then Jeff said, "I've changed my mind. This isn't like *The Cay*. It's like *Gilligan's Island*. We're castaways!"

When we'd calmed down, we ate our dinner. I knew it was the last big meal we would have. We didn't even drink anything with it because I thought we should save our liquids as long as possible.

We sat around the fire. It was cosy—like camping—and everyone seemed relaxed, except me. Mary Anne's words kept running through my head. I hoped she hadn't meant what she'd said. Whether she had or not, I promised myself that in future I would try to be more responsible. Was this disaster a punishment for *not* being responsible? I wondered. Then I began to feel guilty because *I* hadn't spoken to *Mary Anne* for so long. When (if?) I saw her again, I told myself that I would hug her, apologise, and never "not speak to her" again.

9th CHAPTER

Stacey

It's like the old days. I'm back in New York City, and this afternoon I sat for my two favourite NYC charges, Henry and Grace Walker. Only now, since I'm a real member of the BSC again, I have to keep records of my sitting jobs and copy them into the club notebook when I get back to Stoneybrook.

It's a long weekend, so today there were plenty of special things to do, or to go to, with Henry and Grace. In fact, we had trouble deciding how to spend our afternoon, but at long last we chose a street fair not far from their block of flats (which used to be my old block of flats before Mum and Dad got divorced and both moved out).

Anyway, at the street fair there were lots of food stalls....

Ring, ring! My note-keeping was interrupted by the telephone. I made a leap for it (my bedroom in Dad's new flat is on the small side, so it wasn't much of a leap) and got to it before the third ring.

"Hello?" I said, hoping it was my New York best friend, Laine Cummings.

"Stacey? Hi, it's Kristy."

Kristy! She was about the last person I'd expected to hear on the other end of the line. In the first place, I wasn't expecting a long-distance call. In the second place, Kristy and I are good friends and all that, but we don't usually talk on the phone when I'm in New York.

"Hi," I said. "Is anything—"

"Stacey, I've got bad news," Kristy interrupted me. "I thought you should hear about it straight away."

A thousand thoughts ran through my mind. If Kristy was phoning me, that meant that Claudia couldn't. Even though Kristy's the chairman of the BSC—and I assumed this had something to do with our friends and the club—Claudia would call me with bad news. Was Claudia ill or hurt?

"What's happened?" I asked Kristy tightly, and I realised that her voice sounded just as tight as mine.

"Claud and Dawn and the children haven't come back from their race yet."

"Haven't come back," I repeated. "But it's

almost seven o'clock! Shouldn't they have been home hours ago?"

"Well, quite a while ago, at any rate," said Kristy.

"Don't you think it's a good sign that *neither* boat has come back?" I asked. "I mean, if one boat sank, the other could still have returned. So wherever they are, they're together. I bet they're on the island."

"Maybe," replied Kristy doubtfully. "Someone will check that soon. They could have crashed into each other, though. But the really scary thing is the weather we've been having. I don't know what it's like in New York—"

"Cloudy, but not bad," I told her.

"Oh. Well, here it started off nice, as you know, but we've been having showers and storms all afternoon. And we had one *huge* thunderstorm. If Claud and Dawn ran into that storm out on the water . . ."

Kristy didn't finish her sentence and she didn't need to.

"Oh, no!" was all I managed to say.

"I know. It's awful. But the community centre's starting a search, even though it's raining again, and the sky is almost as dark as night-time. They're sending out boats and they've called the Coastguard. Tomorrow, the Coastguard will send out boats. They'll also send up helicopters and other small planes to search from the air. Mal's

73

family is probably going to take some big boats out and look, and the people at the centre say that if Claud and everyone haven't been found by tomorrow, then anyone who wants to can help by walking along the beach, looking for wreckage."

"Ugh!" I said. "That's awful. I don't even want to think about wreckage."

"Listen," Kristy went on, "one reason I'm calling is to let you know that if they *haven't* been found by tomorrow, I'm calling an emergency BSC meeting for the morning. We'll hold it at Mallory's house. Do you think you'd like to come back for it? I know meetings are for discussing babysitting problems, but to me, this—"

"They're also for club problems, aren't they?" I didn't wait for Kristy to answer. I just rushed on. "And this is a club problem. Two of our members are *missing*. I'll definitely try to be there. But I'll have to ask Dad first. And anyway, let's hope they'll have been found by then and we won't need meetings or search planes or anything tomorrow."

"Right," said Kristy, still sounding grim.

Then a thought struck me. "How are Jessi and the Braddocks and the Kishis and everyone doing?"

"As well as can be expected. Jessi'll probably have to phone that aunt of hers, and her parents will probably come home. I haven't talked to her yet, though. It was Mrs Kishi who rang me with the news, and she sounded awful. She was *crying* over the phone." (I hate it when adults cry.) "She's worried about Claud, of course, but I think she also feels responsible for Jamie and Becca, since they were in Claudia's boat. But mostly she just sounded as if she was in shock.

"Then," Kristy continued, "I rang the Newtons to see if they needed me to come and stay with Lucy if they wanted to be at the centre. Lucy's too little to hang around there all night, and none of the BSC members are available except me. You're in New York, Claud and Dawn are, well, wherever, Jessi's stuck at home, Mal's keeping her company, and Mary Anne's keeping her father and step-mother company. That leaves me."

"How did the Newtons sound?" I asked. "Who did you talk to?"

"I couldn't get them. I expect they're already at the centre."

I sighed, thinking of all those distraught families —the Kishis; Dawn's new family, especially Mary Anne; the Braddocks; the Newtons; and the Ramseys.

"Oh, I wish Dawn and Mary Anne had been speaking to each other," I was saying, when there was a knock at my door. "Hang on a second," I told Kristy. "Come in!" I called. Dad came into my room. He tapped his watch to remind me of the time. We had theatre tickets for eight o'clock that night. "Kristy, I have to go, but I'll call you back in a little while, okay?"

"Okay."

I hated to ring off. It was like cutting off my last tie with Stoneybrook . . . and with Claudia.

"Darling," said Dad, sitting on my bed, "it's after seven and you're not dressed yet. We've got to leave in less than half an hour."

"I can't go," I told my father flatly. "I've got to get back to Stoneybrook tonight. It's really important." I told him what had happened.

"You can't leave tonight!" replied my father. "You just got here this morning—and you're staying till Monday."

"But, Dad, these are my *friends*. I have to help find them."

"Stacey, I'm sure nothing horrible has happened to them. Even if there's a big search tomorrow, what can you do? You don't know anything about boats."

"I can go out sailing with the Pikes. Or I can join the search on the shore for the—wreckage."

"I really don't think you need to go," said Dad firmly. "Besides, we've got the theatre tickets and it took me ages to get them. On top of that, I never see you. Well, hardly ever. Well, not as often as I'd like. I miss you."

"And I'll miss Claudia and Dawn if anything's happened to them."

"That's a pretty big 'if', Anastasia," said my father.

Whoa! *Anastasia*: It was time to stop arguing. Dad only uses my full name when he's fed up with me.

"I'll get dressed," I said. I bet my lips were white. That's how angry I was. As soon as Dad had left my room, I closed the door. I'm sure my father thought I just wanted the privacy, but I was *closing him out*.

Then, instead of changing, I rang Kristy to tell her I couldn't come home. Then I rang Laine Cummings and told her the whole story. Every word.

"Claudia and Dawn are *missing*?" she whispered. "Wow! I don't believe it." (Laine knows my Stoneybrook friends.)

"Yes. And Dad won't let me go back to Connecticut."

"That's pretty bad."

"He's just being selfish!" I cried. Then we had to get off the phone, since I really did need to change for the theatre. But while I was getting dressed, all I could think about was my parents' stupid divorce. If they had behaved like grown-ups, worked out their problems, and stayed together, then I wouldn't be a divorced child. I wouldn't be stuck with one parent in one place, while my friends were in trouble in another place. They needed me and I couldn't go to them.

I hate being a divorced child.

10th CHAPTER

Dawn

Looking Back—
Saturday Night
It was funny, but one thing
that scared me a lot that first
night on the island was looking
down and discovering that my
watch had stopped. It wasn't
waterproof and it was ruined.
Oh, no! I thought. We'll never
know what time it is now! Isn't
it weird—- the kinds of things
that worry you? I mean, there
I was, stranded on some island
with a group of kids, and I was
worried because I didn't know
what time it was.

Claudia must have seen the look on my face because she reached over from where she was sitting and put her hand on my arm. "What's wrong?" she asked gently.

"Our watches!" I cried. "They've been ruined by the water. How will we be able to keep time?"

"Don't worry," said my brother. "*My* watch is waterproof." He checked it. "The time," he said grandly, "is exactly nine-oh-two."

I relaxed. I knew the time. And the children and Claud and I were safe, warm, dry, and had full stomachs. Our fire was burning nicely, although we had to put sticks on it all the time to keep it going, and knew we would have to do that throughout the night. We were sitting round the fire in a circle, as if we were at camp. Jamie was in Claudia's lap, though, because we weren't sure he was old enough to know he should stay away from the fire.

We'd been talking for quite a while, the six of us, but it was odd—nobody mentioned our awful predicament. We talked about Kristy's softball team, about a test that Dawn and I would have to do at school the following week, and about what a pest Jamie thought Lucy was.

By the time we found out that it was nine o'clock, though, we were beginning to fade. Jamie was almost asleep in Claudia's arms, and Becca's head was beginning to nod.

79

"I think," I said (and Becca came to), "it's bedtime."

At home, probably any one of us would have given our parents a hard time about going to bed at nine o'clock, but the exhausted castaways agreed with me immediately. We had just one problem.

"What are we going to sleep on?" asked Jeff.

Sitting on the floor of the cave was one thing. Sleeping on it was another. It was dusty and cold, not to mention hard.

"Well," I said, "there's the blanket we packed for our picnic. That's still dry, thanks to Jeff."

Jeff grinned. He'd wrapped it in a tarpaulin and thrown it on to Claud's boat.

In the cave, we'd put the tarpaulin-wrapped items next to the bottled water and Claud's chocolate bars. Now we unrolled each one until we came to the blanket. I spread it on the floor near the fire and Jeff lay down on it.

"Won't do," he said. "It's practically as hard as the cave floor. Just fuzzy. It's like lying on a really, really hard peach."

Becca and Haley giggled.

It took some thinking and experimenting, but we finally hit on the idea of spreading out dry leaves (*not* too close to the fire) and lying on them with the blanket over us. This way we kept warm and were reasonably comfortable.

"Jeff," I said, "can you help Claudia and me

keep the fire going tonight? We could do with some help, and you've gone camping a lot."

"Of course," he replied. Ever since Jeff moved back to California, he's become one of the most easygoing, pleasant people I know.

So we lay under the blanket, with our heads facing the fire, since Claudia said that her grandmother used to say, "Keep your head covered!" whenever it was cold outside. And Becca added that Dr Johanssen had told her that we lose the most body heat through our heads. We lay in this order: me, Jeff, Becca, Haley, Jamie, Claudia.

Before we lay down, we moved our supply of kindling nearer the fire. "But how will we wake up to feed the fire?" I asked. I had a feeling that once the six of us lay down, we'd be out like lights.

"I'll set the alarm on my watch," answered Jeff.

"Are you sure it's working?" asked Claudia.

"No."

"Then maybe we should keep watch," she said. "That might be a good idea in any case."

"What does that mean?" asked Jamie sleepily, and I knew he was confusing "keeping watch" with "wristwatch"

"It means . . . stay awake and make sure that, um, nothing happens. I mean, that we're safe."

"Safe from what?" asked Jamie, sounding more awake.

The six of us were snuggled into our nest, but the children didn't seem so sleepy any more.

"Safe from, oh . . ."

Claudia and I exchanged a Look, wondering how to get out of this mess.

"Bears?" asked Jamie, beginning to cry.

"Poisonous snakes?" asked Haley.

Next to me, even Jeff looked alarmed. "We don't know what's on this island," he said. "Maybe this cave belongs to a—"

I nudged him in the ribs before he could say anything too horrible.

"Maybe it belongs to a monster!" cried Becca.

"Oh, Becca! You don't really believe in monsters, do you?" asked Claud.

"Noooo," she said uncertainly. "But I'm afraid of the dark."

"Me, too," said Jamie, as Claud comforted him.

"Now come on, all of you." I tried to sound cheerful.

There was a silence. Then Haley said, "When will we be rescued?"

"I don't know," I answered honestly, "but I can tell you one thing. Everyone must be searching for us. We were supposed to be home this afternoon. Now it's almost ten o'clock."

"Are they looking for us in the dark?" asked Becca.

Again I had to say, "I don't know." But then I

added, "They'll definitely be looking for us tomorrow."

"Then we can go home tomorrow!" exclaimed Haley.

"Well, only if they *find* us," Claudia pointed out. "We're not sure which island we're on."

"Oh. I see," was Haley's reply.

Another silence followed, and I allowed myself to think: good, they're all going to sleep now.

I was fooled. The moment of silence was just the calm before the storm. Suddenly all four children cried out at once:

"What if a rattlesnake slithers in here and bites us?" asked Haley.

"What if there really *are* monsters?" asked Becca. "Island monsters."

"I'm afraid of my dreams!" exclaimed Jamie.

And Jeff said, "What if we're in Nova Scotia or somewhere? No one will *ever* find us! We're doomed."

Claudia and I started talking fast.

"We can't be *too* far from Stoneybrook," said Claud. "We didn't drift for very long."

"And if we're still near Connecticut, then we don't have to worry about rattlesnakes or other poisonous snakes. There aren't any around here," I pointed out.

"Anyway, the fire will keep animals—and— monsters—away," said Claudia.

"And if you think about nice things, then you'll

83

have nice dreams," I told Jamie. "Now go to sleep, everyone."

After a few minutes, Claud whispered, "Dawn?"

"Yes?"

"Come over for a sec so I can talk to you while the others are sleeping."

I wriggled out from under the blanket, walked round our bed, and sat on the cold ground next to Claudia. "What is it?" I asked.

"We should think about tomorrow," she said.

"Right," I agreed.

"We've only got two options as far as I can see. A couple of us could go out in the boat, or we could wait here to be rescued."

"I suppose. They don't sound like wonderful choices, do they?"

"No," replied Claud uncertainly. "But we don't have to make a decision until tomorrow. We'll see what the weather's like. We'll walk round the island. Maybe we'll even be able to see land from somewhere. If we can, then going out in the boat will make more sense."

We talked for a bit longer. And then, dead tired, I tiptoed back to the other end of the bed. As soon as I got there, Jeff opened his eyes. "Even the people on *Gilligan's Island* were rescued in the end," he whispered.

I grinned. "Go to sleep, Jeff," I said.

11th CHAPTER

Claudia

Looking Back—
Sundy Mourning

I didn't expet the iland to be butiful but
it was. It was very pretty. I realy felt
like a caracter in a storybook. When we
woke up, we looked all around. The wether
had cleered up. The sky was blue agian. The
only clouds were far away. And the kids
were exited. They thot we would be found
that day. Just one scary thing wehn we
woke up. Jeff had gone.

"Where's Jeff?" were the first words I heard the next morning.

Dawn, Jeff, and I had spent the night keeping the fire going. Jeff had had the last watch. Now, as the rest of us woke up, we discovered that he had gone. Dawn was the one who had said, "Where's Jeff?"

I sat up in a hurry. I looked across our bed, which was a huge, leafy mess. There were Jamie, Haley, and Becca sitting up sleepily. And there was Dawn, standing up, looking panicky.

But Becca said, "I saw him tiptoe out of the cave a little while ago."

"Are you sure?" asked Dawn.

"Positive."

"I bet he went exploring," said Becca.

"I hope so," replied Dawn. "I mean, I hope that's all he's doing."

Becca stretched, stood up, and walked to the entrance of the cave. "Gosh," she said. "It's a really nice day, even though it's hazy. But it's cold out there. Our cave is warm."

Dawn joined Becca at the cave entrance. "It *is* a nice day," she agreed. "I bet it'll warm up later. Maybe the haze will die away too."

"You know what? It's almost *too* hot in here," said Jamie, looking flushed.

"It *is* pretty warm," I said. "But we'd better not let the fire go out. We'll be sorry tonight if we do. Besides, we don't have that many matches."

"I wonder what time it is," said Dawn. "My brother's gone out with our only watch. I could ki—I mean, I wish he hadn't done that."

By that time we were all awake. And the more awake the children got, the more excited they became. After last night, I'd expected them to greet the morning with fears, asking when we would be rescued, but Becca was excited about the weather, Haley was excited because she could see the water from the cave entrance, and Jamie dashed around crying, "We can go swimming later! And we've all got our swimsuits with us. Isn't that *great*? Can I go swimming *now*?"

I shook my head. "No. But you can go later. After it's warmed up and after we've eaten our breakfast."

"What's for breakfast?" Haley wanted to know.

Dawn and I exchanged a glance.

"Well," said Dawn, "not very much. You've got a choice. Fruit or chocolate bars. I'm afraid that's it."

The children looked a little bewildered.

Finally Jamie said, "No scrambled eggs?"

"I'm sorry," I told him. "Not unless you find a chicken on the island."

Jamie giggled.

Becca looked thoughtful. At last she said, "I love chocolate bars . . . but I've never had one for breakfast." She also looked a little naughty, as if she'd been told, "You can't have chocolate until

87

after three o'clock in the afternoon," and now she was being given the opportunity of a lifetime. "I'll take the chocolate!" she cried suddenly. I'm sure she thought she'd never have the chance again.

"*Me*, too!" exclaimed Haley.

"*I'll* have a banana," said Dawn.

"Me, too," said Jamie bravely.

"Well, I'm no fool," I said. "I'm going to have a chocolate bar."

"Or you could have fish," spoke up another voice.

We all turned towards the cave entrance. There stood Jeff, looking extremely proud of himself. He was grinning from ear to ear. And in his hands he held out some leaves on which he'd placed three small fish.

"How did you catch those?" asked Dawn, amazed.

"I'll show you later. It was easier than I thought it would be." He held up a stick with a length of string attached to it and an open safety pin tied to the string. I suppose he'd found the things in the survival kit. "I would have caught more, but I thought you'd have woken up and would be wondering where I was."

"We had and we were," said Dawn sternly, and I thought she was going to yell at him. Instead she said, "By the way, what time is it?"

"Nine o'clock," Jeff replied.

"It's always nine o'clock on this island," commented Dawn.

"I think we should name this island," said Jamie. "We'll call it Nine O'Clock Island."

"That's a stupid name," said Haley.

"Hey, come on, all of you," said Dawn. "With any luck, we'll leave the island today and we won't have to worry about naming it. Jeff, could you see land from your fishing spot?".

"No," he replied. "Too hazy."

Dawn sighed. "Oh, well," she said. Then she went on, "Now, look. Jeff's got three fish. We can cook them over the fire and have a nice, healthy breakfast."

"*Fish*?" squeaked Becca. "No way! I'm not eating fish."

"Me, neither," said Haley. "Not at breakfast. Not at any other time."

Dawn looked at Jamie, who'd said he'd eat a banana. I suppose the thought of a banana and fish for breakfast was just too much for him. He changed his mind entirely. "I'll have a chocolate bar!"

In the end, Dawn and Jeff divided the fish, cooking them over the fire, then eating one-and-a-half each (they really were small), while the rest of us ate one chocolate bar each.

"This is good," I said, surveying our food supply as we sat around the fire with our

89

breakfasts. "We still have most of the chocolate bars and the fruit—and Jeff can fish."

"*Now* can I have something to drink?" asked Haley.

"Just a little," replied Dawn. "I've got a feeling that we should save our water and orange juice. You can have half a carton of orange juice, okay?"

"Okay," replied Haley. She ended up sharing a carton with Becca.

Before we'd finished eating, I said, "You know, Jeff, we're very grateful to you for the fish, but when Dawn realised you'd gone, she was really worried. We don't know our way around this island yet and I wouldn't want anybody getting lost. From now on, nobody should go anywhere alone—"

"Except *maybe* Claud or me," added Dawn.

"Right," I said, "and nobody goes *any*where without telling Dawn or me first. Okay?"

"Okay," said Haley, Becca, Jamie, and Jeff.

"And no swimming without a friend and a life jacket," added Dawn.

"A life jacket?" cried Jeff. "Just for *swimming*?"

"Absolutely," replied Dawn. "Claudia and I are responsible for you lot and we aren't taking any chances."

Well, no one was very happy with Dawn and me for laying down rules, but they forgot their anger when Becca brightened suddenly and said, "I've got a *great* idea!"

90

"What?" cried the rest of us.

"Jeff, did you see any shells on the beach when you were fishing?"

"Tons," he replied. "Big ones. Clamshells, maybe. I think they were washed up during the storm yesterday."

"Great," said Becca. "Listen, this is my idea: since people think we're lost at sea, they'll probably be looking for us in boats *and* aeroplanes, right?"

"Right," we agreed.

"And we ought to let them know where we are, right?"

"Yes?" we said tentatively.

"So what we do is collect about a million of those clamshells and use them to spell out HELP as big as we can on the beach. Then people could see our message from the air."

"Becca, that's a terrific idea!" exclaimed Jeff. "Anyone would see that."

I wasn't so sure because of the haze, and I could tell that Dawn wasn't, either.

Becca's brilliant idea sounded like something she'd seen on TV. And she probably had. Seen it, I mean. On the other hand, Dawn and I hadn't come up with any better ideas. None that we wanted to try just yet anyway.

So we let the children get carried away with enthusiasm. As soon as the day had warmed up, we stripped off our clothes (we were wearing our swimsuits underneath) and plastered on suntan oil. Then, keeping my promise to Mrs Newton, I made Jamie put on his windcheater. When we were ready, we followed Jeff to the beach near his fishing hole and found the "tons" of clamshells.

"Oh, boy!" exclaimed Becca.

"Let's get to work," added Haley.

And so we began our first attempt at getting rescued.

12th CHAPTER

Kristy

Sunday Morning —
Emergency Meeting

Today was the first meeting of the BSC ever held at Mallory's house. (I took notes on it since this is a dire situation, and anyway, I am the chairman.) It was not a happy meeting. Two of our members are missing, and I mean actually missing, and a third member was absent. Stacey had called to say that her father wouldn't let her come home straight away. She sounded really angry. We felt sorry for her and wished she was with us, but we were more concerned with other things. Like — exactly where Dawn, Claudia, Jamie, Jeff, Becca, and Haley are.

Kristy

We've never held a meeting at the Pikes' house. In fact, I don't think we've held a Stoneybrook meeting anywhere except in Claudia's room. We held them there when we were angry with each other and conducted meetings one person at a time so we wouldn't have to look at each other's faces. We held them there when Claudia was all caught up with this new friend of hers, Ashley Wyeth, and kept missing meetings. We even held them there straight after Claudia's grandmother had died, because Claud had said she wanted her life to go on as normally as possible.

The point is, a meeting in Mal's room seemed very, very odd. She hasn't got a phone, but that didn't matter since we weren't arranging jobs. We were trying to decide what we could do to help find our vice-chairman, our alternate officer, and four children we like a lot. The absence of Claud and Dawn was profound. (I read that word in a book and I really like it.) The absence of Stacey was noticeable, of course, but since we knew where she was, it didn't seem profound (at least not to me).

The four remaining members tried to make ourselves comfortable in the room that Mal shares with her sister Vanessa. Since there are two beds in the room, and only four of us were at the meeting, we were all able to sit on beds for once. Mallory and I sat on one of the twin beds; Mary Anne and Jessi, looking absolutely awful, sat on the other. I don't think I've ever seen either of them so shaken up.

Mallory and I were pretty upset ourselves. I even found it difficult to be official. So I didn't start the meeting by calling it to order. I just said, "Okay, everyone, this is an emergency meeting."

Before I could say anything more, Mary Anne, in her upset, said, "Oh, my gosh! I haven't got any paper or a pencil. How am I supposed to take notes?" She was practically crying.

"Don't worry about it," I told her. "I'll take care of it." Mal handed me a notebook and a pen, and I started writing and talking at the same time, which isn't easy to do.

"All right," I went on. "As I said, this is an emergency meeting. Claudia and Dawn are still missing."

At that point, Mary Anne really did begin to cry. She let loose a flood of tears, which set Jessi off. Mal and I were slightly surprised. Mary Anne cries at the drop of a hat, but Jessi hardly ever does.

Mal ran into the bathroom, came back with a box of tissues, and handed a huge bunch to Mary Anne. She took some and passed the rest around.

"Anything could have happened to them!" wailed Mary Anne, and we all knew who she meant by "them". "Their boats could have capsized in that storm. They could have—"

95

Kristy

"SHHH!" I nudged her in the ribs. "Jessi's *sister* is missing!" I hissed.

"Well, so's mine," replied Mary Anne, sniffling.

Oh, yes. Sometimes I forget that Dawn and Mary Anne are stepsisters now, even though I've got a stepsister of my own.

"And," Mary Anne continued in a wobbly voice, "I bet Jessi didn't tell *her* sister she never wanted to see her again. I didn't mean that when I said it. Do you think this is some sort of punishment for being such an awful sister?"

"No," Mal, Jessi, and I said at the same time.

"You don't?" replied Mary Anne.

"Of course not," I said. "We all say things we don't mean."

"Like the time Nicky wished the triplets would turn into pigs," added Mal. "Do you think that actually happened?"

"No," said Mary Anne. "But this seems like more than coincidence."

"Well, did you say you wished you'd never see Claudia, Haley, Becca, Jeff, or Jamie again?" I asked sensibly.

"No," Mary Anne answered. "Still . . . if yesterday really *was* the last time I saw my sister—I mean, um, alive—I'll feel terrible."

Jessi's sobs grew louder.

"Okay, you lot," I said sternly. (I felt awful being stern in these circumstances, but somebody had to do it.) "I know the situation doesn't look

96

very good, but would everyone be out searching if they really thought that Dawn and Claud were—I mean, if they really thought there was no point?"

"No," said Jessi and Mary Anne feebly.

"Absolutely not," said Mal, and I gave her a thank-you smile.

"Well, that's why we're here today," I went on. "What can we do to help search? Or at least to help the Newtons and the Braddocks and the Kishis and everyone through this difficult time?"

"How *are* the Newtons and the Braddocks and the Kishis doing?" asked Mal.

"About as well as my dad and stepmother and Jessi's family are," replied Mary Anne. "And about as well as Mr Schafer would be doing if he knew what was going on, but he doesn't. We can't reach him. I think he's away for the long weekend."

Jessi groaned. "You know what?" she said. "Sorry this is on a different subject, Kristy, but I must tell you. Mum and Dad are on their way home."

"Oh," moaned Mal. "Their holiday's been ruined."

"Yes. And Aunt Cecelia's taken over our house completely. She's looking after Squirt, and for some reason, she's cleaning like a demon. You'd think she'd be out searching."

"The Braddocks, the Newtons, and the Kishis

97

are searching," added Mary Anne. "My mum spoke to Mrs Newton, Mr Braddock, and both of Claud's parents last night. Someone's looking after Lucy Newton all day today, and Mr and Mrs Newton are out on a Coastguard boat. The Braddocks are combing the shore for any sign of debris and even Matt's joined in. The Kishis are there too. And my dad and Sharon are helping coordinate things at the centre. I think the searching and helping is a sort of therapy. It stops everyone going crazy."

"So what can we do?" I asked for the fifty millionth time.

"*I* want to go out on a boat and search, but there's no way Aunt Cecelia will let me do that," said Jessi. "I'm already in hot water with her. She thinks I'm the one to blame, even though Mama and Daddy gave Becca permission to go sailing. She's so unfair. I hate my aunt."

"So you're stuck here," I said. "Do you think your aunt would let you search along the beach?"

Jessi sighed. "I don't know. I don't want to be at home with that—that old *bat*." (I almost giggled.) "On the other hand, she nearly stopped me coming here, so she probably won't let me help search."

"What about you, Mal?" I asked.

"Oh, I'll be out on a big motorboat with my parents and probably the triplets by this afternoon. We've cancelled our plans so that we can go searching. It won't be easy trying to see through this awful haze, but any of you can join us. It seems as though practically all of Stoneybrook is looking for Claud and Dawn and Becca and everyone."

For some reason, tears came to my eyes then. I don't cry much. In fact, I'm the opposite of Mary Anne. But every now and then something gets to me. Suddenly I was thinking of all the families— the distraught parents, the bewildered brothers and sisters—and I couldn't control it. Mallory handed *me* some tissues, and then had to grab some for herself. I suppose the sight of the rest of us crying was too much for her. She hugged Jessi, and I hugged Mary Anne.

After several minutes, Mary Anne blew her nose and said, "I just don't think I can help with the search. It might be therapy, but I wouldn't be able to keep my mind on it. I know it's childish, but all I can think of are the horrible things I said to Dawn."

"And Stacey won't be able to help," I added as my tears dried. "Not unless her father lets her come back from New York."

"What about you, Kristy?" asked Mallory. "Do you want to come out in the boat with my family? We'd be glad to have you."

I started to say, "Of course" when I remembered something. "Uh-oh!" I said instead. I felt my face flush.

99

"What?" asked the others.

"I've just remembered. I've arranged a Krushers' practice for this afternoon."

"Cancel it," said Mal.

"I can't. I mean, it's not that easy. We've got a game tomorrow. We arranged it for the Monday holiday, and the Krushers have really been looking forward to it. They think they might *finally* beat the Bashers. I think so, too. I'd hate to let them down. I've got responsibilities to them."

"You've got responsibilities to your friends, too," said Jessi softly.

"You're right," I replied. Then I paused. "I don't know what to do. It's not fair to let the children down. The boating disaster doesn't have anything to do with them, except that Haley and Jamie won't be at the game."

"Are you sure it's not Bart you're afraid of letting down?" asked Mary Anne. She always manages to get to the heart of the matter where matters of the heart are concerned. You see, I go out with Bart Taylor sometimes. He just happens to be the Bashers' coach.

I thought for a moment. At last I said, "You know what? You're right, Mary Anne. I don't want Bart to think I'm chickening out. And that's about the worst reason I can come up with for not going with Mal today. I'll ring Bart and cancel tomorrow's game. Then I'll ask Sam or someone to help me cancel the Krushers' practice for today."

"Let's give Stacey one more call to see if she can come home early," suggested Mary Anne.

So we did, but she couldn't.

After that I rang Sam to ask him to give me a hand with cancelling practice.

And *then* I picked up the phone (in private) to call Bart.

13th CHAPTER

Dawn

Looking Back —
Late Sunday Morning

You know what was wrong with spelling HELP with shells? The shells were about the same colour as the sand. Claudia and I realized early on in the project that no one would be able to see our message, especially from as far away as up in a plane. The only thing a search plane would see was a stretch of white at the edge of an island. Even from down the beach, Claud and I couldn't tell the clam shells from the sand. But we didn't let the kids know that. We simply realized that if we were going to be rescued, we'd have to work harder, or do something more drastic....

Well, if nothing else, spelling out our message put the children in good spirits. So did the planes we could hear, but not see through the fog and haze. The children were sure we'd be rescued later that day.

"We're working really hard!" Jamie yelled to Claud and me at one point.

"That's terrific!" I shouted back.

The reason we were shouting was that Claud and I were finishing the H and Jamie was finishing the P, and our all-white disaster signal was so big we were pretty far apart.

"And guess what!" Jamie went on.

"What?" yelled Claud.

"Now I know how to spell *six* words: Jamie, Lucy, Mummy, Daddy, love, and *help*!"

Jamie roared the last word, and the rest of us laughed. Despite what Claudia and I had realised about our message, even the two of us were in better spirits. It was funny, but in spite of our *awful* predicament we weren't feeling too bad at that point. Wandering along an island beach in our swimsuits was pleasant. We were almost able to forget that we were castaways.

When HELP was finally finished (and it took a long time to do) the children wanted to do the things they'd missed out on the afternoon before —namely swim, explore (cautiously), play games, and, now, learn to fish.

"I just want you to know," Haley made a point

of telling Claudia and me as she was about to go to Jeff's fishing spot, "that I *still* won't eat fish. Not now, not ever."

"That's okay," Claud told her. "I'm not keen on fish myself. Especially when I see them alive before I eat them."

I rolled my eyes.

Claudia and I played lifeguard for about an hour while Becca swam in the sea and patiently tried to teach Jamie the sidestroke. Jamie worked hard but it's difficult to learn the sidestroke when you're wearing a life jacket. He kept rolling over. At least he and Becca thought that was funny. Becca finally started pretending that Jamie was her pet puppy. She'd shriek, "Roll over!" and Jamie would because he couldn't help it.

Claudia and I laughed until we ached.

"I wonder what time it is," I said as we got our breaths back.

Claud looked at me as though I was crazy. "Why are you always so worried about what the time is?" she asked. Then she quickly added, "I bet it isn't nine o'clock."

I smiled. "I'm just wondering how long the children have been in the water. It isn't all that warm."

"Oh, you're right," said Claud. "Hey, Becca! Jamie! Come on back here!"

Reluctantly, our two swimmers waded ashore.

Jamie's lips were blue and his teeth were chattering.

"Uh-oh!" said Claud. "I promised Mrs Newton I'd keep Jamie warm. Here, Jamie. Put on your windcheater."

"Yuck!" said Jamie. But he put it on anyway.

At that point, Haley and Jeff returned, looking pretty proud of themselves.

"Lunch!" Jeff called, dramatically holding out several more small fish for Claud and me to see.

"Yum!" I said.

"Ugh!" Claud said.

"Wimp!" I teased her.

"Dawn? Can we build a fort?" asked Jeff, after checking his watch for me. "You know, we might need one. The cave is good shelter, but it's rather damp and cold. And we don't know how long we're going to be—"

Jeff stopped when I gave him a look.

"You mean building a fort might be lots of fun?" said Claud.

"Oh. Yes," said Jeff.

"Of course you can," I told the children. All four of them were crowded around, waiting for an answer.

"Great!" they cried.

"But stay right at the edge of the woods where we can see you," said Claud.

The children ran off, and Claudia and I sat

105

down by a boulder. We watched Jeff instruct the others on fort building.

"He's really good with children," Claud remarked after a while.

"I know," I said. "I discovered that the last time I was staying in California. Jeff and I were babysitting for two children one night, and the baby wouldn't stop crying. So I looked after the baby and Jeff entertained the older child. He was great."

"It's good to know," said Claud slowly. "I mean, if anything happens to you or to me, I think Jeff could sort of take over."

I didn't answer. The thought was too frightening.

We watched as the fort building continued. The children were having a lot of fun, but they weren't making much progress.

"You know," Claudia said as Haley and Becca tried to lash some sticks together with damp vines, "we're just putting it off."

"Putting what off?" I asked.

"Finding the boat."

I sighed. "Yes."

"Because when we find it," Claud went on, "we'll have to decide what to do. Whether to send a couple of people off in it or not."

I sighed again. Then I said, "Let's go right now."

"Now?"

"Why not? The children aren't near the water and I trust Jeff to be in charge. If I tell him to keep the others out of the water and not to go any further into the woods than they are now, he'll do what I say."

"Okay." Claud got to her feet and dusted the sand off her swimsuit.

"Jeff?" I shouted.

"Yes?"

"Come here for a sec."

Jeff ran across the beach to Claud and me. He listened seriously as I told him what we were going to do. Then he promised to keep the others entertained and to follow my instructions.

So Claudia and I set off down the beach. We walked and walked.

"I don't remember coming this far yesterday," I said after a while.

"Neither do I," said Claudia. "You know what? I think we've come too far. I don't remember that gnarled tree." She pointed towards the woods.

"Maybe we went in the wrong direction," I suggested.

"No. I'm sure we went the right way."

Claudia and I had walked about half way back to the children when the same thought struck us at the same time.

"Oh, no!" whispered Claudia.

"The boat's washed away, hasn't it?" I said.

"It must have done. I bet we landed at low tide." Claudia smacked her hand to her forehead. "How could we have been so stupid?"

"We didn't know," I pointed out. "We didn't know it was low tide."

"Yes, but we should at least have pulled the boat inland a little."

"Well, we didn't."

"Now what?" asked Claud. "That boat was the only way for us to leave the island."

"Not a very good way, though. Not safe. And we can't see land because of this awful haze. Why won't the weather clear up? No one will be able to see us, will they?"

"No," admitted Claudia.

"So we couldn't have sailed off. We wouldn't have known where we were going. We would probably have ended up adrift."

Claudia sank down in the sand.

"What? What is it?" I asked, sitting beside her.

"I just thought of something. Your boat got wrecked yesterday. I think we can be sure of that. And my boat just floated away. I'm sure people are out searching today, but when they find one wrecked boat and one empty boat, what will they think?"

"The worst," I replied.

Claudia nodded. "Oh, I hope they don't stop searching."

"I bet they won't. Not right away," I said.

But Claudia didn't believe me. Even *I* didn't believe me. And although I'm usually known for being calm and unflappable, I burst into tears there on the beach. I cried and cried. Claudia tried to comfort me, but at that moment, it was impossible. All my guilt over Mary Anne came flowing out, along with about a hundred other worries including, of course, our predicament.

"Dawn," said Claudia finally, "we must go back to the children."

"I know."

"And they'll get upset if they see that you're upset."

"I know."

"Can you stop crying?"

"Yes," I replied, and I did.

We walked along the beach and found Jeff leading Haley, Becca, and Jamie in a game of tag. He ran to us as soon as he saw us.

"What did you find?" he asked.

I told him.

"Too bad," he said, frowning. Then he pointed to the sky. "I don't want to scare anyone, but ..."

I looked up. Another storm was brewing.

14th CHAPTER

Mary Anne

Sunday Afternoon

I'd forgotten that I had a sitting job with Charlotte Johanssen this afternoon. Completely forgotten. And I'd arranged it myself, since I'm the club secretary. Luckily Dr Johanssen phoned me about an hour before the job, wondering if I still wanted to babysit. She knew that Claud and Dawn and everyone were missing (the whole town knew it), and that I might want to search instead of sitting.

Mary anne

*But I decided to baby sit.
I hoped it would take
my mind off both the disaster
and my problems with Logan....*

As you can imagine, Dad and my stepmother were nearly hysterical about Dawn and Jeff. Sharon wasn't just worried that her children were missing. She also kept saying things like, "Oh, they're going to take custody away from me and I'll never see Dawn again. Jeff will never even be allowed to visit me here." And Dad kept saying things like, "It's not your fault."

At least Sharon thought that everyone would be found. Even so, she continued to make frantic calls to Mr Schafer in California. He wasn't at home, though. And if he had an answering machine, it wasn't on. We had no idea where he was.

When I got home from our emergency BSC meeting, Dad and Sharon had gone. They were at the community centre.

What was I going to do with myself for the rest of the day? I wondered. I was beginning to feel guilty about not searching. Just then the phone rang.

News! I thought. (That was what I'd thought every time the phone had rung since last night.)

I raced for the phone. "Hello?" I said breathlessly.

111

"Mary Anne?"

Logan?! No, it couldn't be.

"This is Logan," said Logan.

I was speechless. Logan and I hadn't talked to each other since our fight. I'd been too cowardly to call him, and I was certain he was too angry to call me.

"Are you there?" asked Logan.

"Oh. Oh, yes," I said brightly.

"Look, I just wanted to say that I'm really sorry about the boating, um, the boating . . ."

It was funny, but nobody really knew what to call the tragedy, since we didn't know what had happened. The Boating Mystery? The Case of the Missing Boaters?

"Thanks," I replied. Was Logan making up with me? Or was he just being polite and concerned? After all, he's a member of the BSC, and he knows Claud and Dawn pretty well. He sees them at school every day.

"Any news?" he asked.

"No." My voice wobbled.

"Are you going to help search?"

"I don't think so. You know I'm no good in . . . I don't know." I didn't feel like telling Logan that Dawn and I hadn't been speaking to each other, either. Then I made up a huge lie. "I thought," I said, "that I'd stay here in case anyone needed me. The Braddocks and the other families are torn to pieces over this." (Well, that much was the truth.) "Someone might need a babysitter . . . Logan?"

"Yes?"

"Does this mean our fight is over?"

"Does what mean our fight is over?"

"This phone call," I said. "You're speaking to me."

There was a long pause. "No. It doesn't."

I felt a rock forming in my stomach. I *hate* it when people are angry with me. "Why not?" I knew I sounded pathetic.

"Because I *still* can't believe that you thought I'd stood you up. I'd never do that. And if you don't know that, then you don't know *me* very well."

Uh-oh! What had I walked into? "I'm sorry," I said.

"Me, too," answered Logan.

And then he rang off.

I'd already cried so much about Dawn and Claudia that I didn't have any tears left in me. Under ordinary circumstances, Logan's hanging up on me would have been a terrific opportunity for a good cry. But I couldn't do it.

I stared into space for a while.

I found Tigger, pulled him into my lap, and patted him for a bit.

I tried ringing Mr Schafer again, but couldn't reach him (again.)

I thought about cleaning the house, but decided

I wasn't quite that desperate. So I went back to staring into space.

That had been going on for fifteen minutes or so when Dr Johanssen rang. "Are you *sure* you want to babysit this afternoon?" she asked.

"Positive," I replied. "I need something to do." Something other than staring.

"I'll warn you. This isn't going to be an easy job. Charlotte's very upset about Becca. We tried to get her to come to Mr Johanssen's company picnic with us, but she looked at us as if we were crazy."

"Well, she and Becca *are* pretty close," I said. "Anyway, don't worry. Charlotte and I will be fine."

"All right," said Dr Johanssen uncertainly.

An hour later I was ringing the Johanssens' bell.

Charlotte answered the door, looking as listless as an old rag.

"Hi," I said.

"Any news?" was Charlotte's reply.

I shook my head. "I'm sorry." Dad and Sharon hadn't even called by the time I'd left the house. (I'd left a gigantic note in the kitchen where they couldn't miss it. The note said I was babysitting for Charlotte. I didn't want them to think that I was missing, too.)

"Come on inside," said Mr Johanssen from behind Charlotte.

114

And for some reason, those words made Charlotte burst into tears.

"Oh, sweetheart!" said her father. He gave her a hug as I edged into the house. "I bet they'll find Becca today. I bet they'll find everyone."

"She's my best friend," wailed Charlotte.

"I know she is. And I know you're worried. Everyone's searching."

"That's right," I told Charlotte. "And not just the Coastguard. The Kishis and the Braddocks and the Newtons and my friends. They're all looking. The Pikes and Kristy even went out on a big boat."

Charlotte's tears subsided.

"Are you sure you don't want to come on the picnic with us?" asked Mr Johanssen. "It would take your mind off—"

"No," interrupted Charlotte, "and I don't know how you can go, either."

Whoa! If I'd said that to Dad . . . big trouble! But the Johanssens just said goodbye to us and left. Charlotte and I were still standing by the front door. She looked at me with huge eyes.

"Hey, Char," I said, inspired, "would you feel better if you could see the search that's going on?"

Charlotte shrugged. "I've seen it on TV."

I'd seen the broadcasts, too. We were on the news. The local networks were covering nothing but the search, and little old Stoneybrook had even made the national news. The local channels called the tragedy the *Connecticut Disaster*. They stationed round-the-clock reporters at the centre, on the beach, and even on the Coastguard boats. They interviewed everyone and kept asking them how they felt. One of them had made the mistake of asking Sharon how she felt, now that two of her children were missing. Guess what she replied? She snapped, "How do you *think* I feel?"

I hadn't seen her on the *Connecticut Disaster* coverage yet.

"Look," I said to Charlotte, "I've seen the search on TV, too, but somehow I have a feeling that's not the same thing. Let's look at it from close up. Do you feel like riding your bike to the community centre?"

"It's a long ride," said Charlotte slowly, but I could tell she was warming to the idea.

"Come on. Get your bike. I rode mine over here."

Well . . . okay!" Charlotte looked as though she wanted to be excited about our adventure, but didn't think she ought to be. Was she afraid of having fun while her best friend was missing? Probably.

We rode to the community centre, taking the fastest route I knew. On the way, we passed a television van.

"Ooh!" said Charlotte. "There are the news-people."

116

When we got hear the centre, we saw that it was so crowded with searchers and families and "newspeople" that we had to chain our bikes to a lamppost two streets away and walk to all the excitement.

"Wow! Look up there!" exclaimed Charlotte just as we reached the centre.

I looked up—and saw two small planes taking off.

"You see?" I said. "They really are doing everything they can to find Becca and the others."

Charlotte nodded, awed.

"There's my dad," I said to Charlotte as we opened the doors.

Dad looked up as we entered the crowded room, but he couldn't talk to me. He was busy on the phone. He waved to me, though. I think he was glad I'd come.

"Let's go out to the quay," I suggested.

And just then a microphone was thrust in front of Charlotte and me. "Are you friends of the missing?" asked a deep voice. It belonged to a TV reporter.

Charlotte and I looked at each other. "Yes," I answered in a small voice.

"And how do you feel right now?" he went on.

I drew myself up. "How do you *think* we feel?" I replied.

The man backed off and Charlotte had to bite her lips to keep from laughing.

117

As soon as we were outside on the docks I said to Charlotte, "I just ruined our chance to be on television. I hope you don't mind."

Charlotte shook her head. "You were great!" she cried.

I was glad I'd done one great thing that day.

Charlotte and I stayed on the dock until about a half an hour before her parents were due back. We saw planes flying low overhead. We saw Coastguard boats and volunteer search boats. We even saw the Pikes and Kristy. They docked late in the afternoon. Everyone got off the boat looking discouraged. Mallory was crying.

"We didn't see anything. Not a thing," she said. Her mother gave her a quick hug.

"Well," I said quickly, "I think that's a good sign. Don't you, Kristy? At least you didn't find any wreckage."

"Yes," agreed Kristy. "No news is good news."

"Right." I squeezed Charlotte's hand. "Come on. We'd better get going."

Charlotte and I rode home silently, each thinking our own thoughts. I know we were impressed by the search efforts. But we were disappointed and worried by the lack of news.

15th CHAPTER

Dawn

Looking Back—
Sunday Afternoon and Night

As long as I live, I hope I never have to go through another night like Sunday night. I know this sounds dramatic, but I truly think it was the most desperate one I've ever spent. Not only hadn't we been rescued, but our food was just about gone and we had a sick child on our hands. Exactly what we needed. Claudia and I dragged up everything we knew about first aid, but there wasn't much we could do without medicine, a thermometer, or ice. What we really needed was a phone so that we could call a doctor.

By the end of Sunday, everyone was flagging. The children had been in high spirits earlier, but now their spirits had dropped right down into the dumps. They were tired of fishing and exploring and swimming and building huts. They were even tired of chocolate bars, which I took as a very bad sign.

At about five o'clock (Jeff Schafer time) we went back to the cave. We'd been running to and from it all day—getting food, escaping from rain, keeping the fire going—but I knew that this would be our final trip there for the day. The children and Claudia looked exhausted. I'm sure I did, too.

"I think we're going to have a nice sunset," said Jeff, trying to sound cheerful.

I looked at the sky. It had been cloudy, then just hazy, then cloudy, then hazy all afternoon. And we'd had a tremendous thunderstorm about twenty minutes after Jeff had pointed out the dark clouds that morning. But now the sky was clear. And the sun was sinking. We would probably have a nice sunset.

"You know what?" said Haley, who was lagging behind.

"What?" I asked, turning round.

"I think it's odd that we haven't been rescued yet. Why hasn't anyone found us?"

"Because they just haven't," answered Claudia before I could say anything.

120

"Then something's wrong. How far from Greenpoint do you think we are?"

"I honestly don't know," said Claud.

"Hey, where's our boat?" asked Jamie crossly. He'd said he was too tired to walk, so Jeff was giving him a piggyback ride.

Claudia and I exchanged a nervous glance.

"It's sort of gone," I replied.

"What do you mean?" asked Becca, narrowing her eyes at me. "How could it be *sort of* gone?"

"Okay, it's completely gone," I told the children. "It washed away during the night. We should have dragged it further up the—"

And right then and there, quiet, sensible, mature Haley threw a temper tantrum. She'd been standing near the cave entrance when she dropped to her knees and began pounding the sand with her fists. "Get the boat back! Get the boat back!" she screeched.

"Haley—" began Claudia.

Jamie finished her sentence for her. "Go to your room," he commanded, but his voice sounded weak. And he looked only mildly interested in Haley.

The rest of us trooped into the cave, leaving Haley and her temper outside to cool off.

Becca was still giving Claudia and me angry looks, so I said to her, "We couldn't have used the boat anyway. Six of us can't fit in it, and besides, we wouldn't know what direction to take if we sailed away. We'd just have got lost. At least we've got shelter on the island . . . Did you hear that, Haley?" I shouted.

"Yes," she replied, stepping guiltily into the cave.

"Gosh! He is warm," said Jeff, letting Jamie slip off his back and down to the ground. "He's like a hot-water bottle."

Claudia and I turned away from Haley and Becca and looked at Jamie. His face was flushed, his eyes were bright, and he seemed awfully tired.

In an instant, Claud and I had both put our hands on Jamie's forehead.

"He's got a temperature," said Claud.

"A high one," I added. "How high do you think it is?"

"A hundred and three?" guessed Claudia.

I nodded.

"Oh no!" said Jeff.

"Jamie? Do you feel all right?" I asked him carefully. I didn't want to put any ideas in his head.

"Not really," he replied.

"What's wrong?" asked Claud.

"I hurt. I hurt all over. Especially my head. And my throat is sore. And my ear aches."

Claud and I glanced at each other over the top of Jamie's head.

"What do you think's wrong with him?" I wondered.

122

" 'Flu?" suggested Claudia.

"Maybe. Do you get earache with 'flu? I hope it isn't an ear infection."

Claudia sighed. "Okay," she said. "Jamie, you're going to have a special bed tonight. Over here, away from the others. Dawn and I will stay with you."

"Thank you," said Jamie politely, and as soon as a "bed" had been prepared for him, he sank on to it and fell asleep.

"What's for dinner?" asked Becca a little while later.

"Fish!" said Jeff.

"Chocolate bars," said Claudia.

The children looked a bit green at the thought of both possibilities.

"Hey," said Claud, "come on. There are three chocolate bars left. We can divide them up. . . . Mmm. Mars bars. Yummy."

But the thought of *more* chocolate was too much for the children. And the thought of fish still put them off, even after Jeff had cooked some for himself and for me.

"It's their *eyes*," said Becca. "How can you bear to look them in the eye, then fry them and *eat* them?"

"Because we'd rather do that than be hungry," replied Jeff.

But Becca, Haley and Claudia chose hunger rather than fish that night. And Jamie, whose stomach was empty, too, just drifted in and out of sleep while the others talked, scared themselves with ghost stories, and played word games.

Claudia and I sat worrying on either side of the sleeping Jamie.

"What should we do?" asked Claud at one point, her hand on his cheek. "He feels warmer than ever. Golly! What I wouldn't give for some children's medicine right now! Or better still, a doctor."

"Maybe he's got a virus," I said. "You know, you're supposed to be able to flush a virus out of someone with water."

Claudia looked sceptical. "I don't know about that," she said, "but if he's got a fever, then he *should* have liquids. That's one thing we can do for him."

"You're right!" I cried. "And we've still got all the bottled water. I had a feeling we should be saving that." I jumped up, got the water and also the remaining cartons of orange juice, and brought them to Jamie's nest. "I think we should wake him up and make him have a drink. We should probably do that all night."

"We'll use up all the water that way," said Claud.

I paused. "I know," I said finally, "but it's the only thing we can do for him."

So we woke up poor Jamie and made him drink about half a cup of water.

124

"It's good for you," I told him.

Jamie coughed and went back to sleep. About an hour later he woke up. "Dawn?" he said, "I'm freezing," and he began to shiver violently.

"Great!" said Claud. "Now he's got a temperature *and* a chill . . . Hey, you lot!" she called to the others, who were getting ready to go to sleep. "I hate to say this, but we need your blanket over here."

It's to their credit that the other children immediately gave up the blanket. Then they inched closer to the fire and burrowed under the leaves. It was the best they could do. Not one of them complained. And Jeff even said, "Call me if you need me," before he drifted off to sleep.

The longest night of my life had begun.

I sat with Jamie while Claud slept a little. Then I woke Jamie up to give him some more water.

"Oh!" he cried. "Stay away!" I had a feeling he didn't mean me. Sure enough, the next words out of his mouth were, "It's a tiger! It's a tiger!"

I gave him the water anyway. When he had finished drinking, he kicked off the blanket. "I'm so *hot*," he murmured, but soon he was shivering again. We needed *half* a layer of blanket.

"Stop! Snake!" Jamie cried out.

"Claud, wake up," I whispered.

"Mmm." She rolled over sleepily.

"I think Jamie's delirious."

125

That woke her up. "What?" she said, sitting up. "Delirious?"

"He's crying out in his sleep. Stuff about tigers and snakes."

"Maybe he's just dreaming."

"I hope so," I said. "How can you tell the difference?"

"I don't know."

"Claud? What if we catch this from Jamie? What are the others going to do if we both get ill?"

Claudia thought for a moment. She rubbed her eyes. "Do you think Jeff can manage the little children all by himself. He *is* pretty responsible."

"Yes, I think he could manage them. Uh oh! What if the children get ill? All of them? Can we look after four children? Or what if—"

"Dawn, stop thinking about the 'what-ifs'. You're driving me crazy. Really. And you're overlooking something important."

"What?"

"We might get rescued. We could all be home by tomorrow night."

Home. Where there were doctors and mothers.

"You know what I want more than anything just now?" I whispered.

Claudia shook her head.

"My mum," I said.

"Me, too."

But we couldn't have our mums, so I slept for a bit. I woke up when Jamie began shrieking about

126

snoring trees. I gave him some water. Then Claudia had a sleep. All night, we took turns sleeping, keeping the fire going, and caring for Jamie. I didn't think our patient was getting any better, though.

16th CHAPTER

Claudia

Looking Back —
Mondy Mornig

The frist thing I did wehn I woke up on mondy was fell Jamie's forhead. It was much cooler I felt releeved. I hopped the worst was over becuase we had no more water left for anyboddy. There was nothing to drink! Even our coke wa gone. I almost paniced. Then I thoght, well mabe we can colect rain water somehow. But do you know why that was a scary thoght? Becuase it meant we had to survive now realy survive. And that meant hard work and use our breians Also we needed some luck.

At six o'clock on Monday morning (I knew it was six because Dawn tiptoed over to her brother and looked at his watch), Dawn said, "I'm exhausted. Can you stay up for a while, Claud?"

I was just waking up. "Of course," I replied groggily.

"Good," said Dawn. She immediately rolled over and fell asleep.

That was when I felt Jamie's forehead.

"Oh, good," I said aloud. "Much cooler."

Jamie was sleeping peacefully. He hadn't cried out for several hours. Maybe the worst was over. And maybe, just maybe, you really could flush a virus out of someone. After all, he'd drunk two whole bottles of water and had been to the toilet about six times.

I tiptoed to the cave entrance. The sky was still grey, but I could see that it was grey with looming clouds as well as with dawn. Great! I thought. Another storm was coming. We needed another storm like we needed extra feet.

"Claudia?" whispered Becca from her nest.

"Yes?" I knelt beside her.

"Is Jamie okay?"

"He's much better. Don't worry about him. Are you okay?" I had taken one of Becca's hands, and it was freezing.

"Just a little cold," said Becca. "I think I'll go back to sleep."

"Sorry about the blanket," I said.

129

"That's okay. Jamie needs it."

Becca nestled under the leaves and fell asleep.

For the next hour, I pottered around the cave. We'd been careful to keep our rubbish in one place so that we wouldn't litter the island. I actually tidied our rubbish! I bet even Mary Anne's tidy, precise father has never tidied rubbish. Then I stoked the fire again, thought about escaping from the island, and checked Jamie. He was still cooler than last night. I didn't think his temperature was normal, but it wasn't anything to be too concerned about.

About an hour later, everyone began to get up.

The first words out of Jeff's mouth were, "I don't believe it. It's *Monday*. This is one of my days off school and look how I'm spending it!"

"Yes, what a holiday!" grumbled Haley. She sat up and brushed the leaves out of her hair, but she missed one. It was sitting on top of her head.

Becca burst into giggles. She pointed to Haley's head. But Haley's only response was to flick the leaf away angrily.

Jeff, who had rarely complained since we landed on "Nine O'Clock Island," now said, "And apart from missing my holiday, I'm freezing. This cave is like a fridge."

"I'll put some more stuff on the fire," I told him quickly.

"Put our bed on it," grumbled Jeff. "It's

useless. We might as well be sleeping on the floor. The leaves don't do a thing."

"I will *not* put your bed on the fire," I told him. "Maybe we can work out a way to make it more comfortable."

That made Becca start to cry.

"What's wrong?" I asked her. I put my arm round her shoulders.

"You mean we're still going to be here to*night*? We're going to need this bed *again*?"

Oops! "No," I answered. "I mean, maybe. We don't know. But just in case."

Becca nodded, sniffling.

"Well, who's hungry?" I asked.

Of course, Becca, Haley, and I were starving. We hadn't eaten since our lunchtime chocolate bars. Worse than that, we were thirsty.

"Couldn't we have just a *little* of Jamie's water?" begged Haley.

"I'd like to let you have some, but it's gone," I said. "He finished it a couple of hours ago. For what it's worth, he seems better."

Becca actually began to wring her hands. "But what are we going to drink? People need liquids. I know that from my science lessons. And we've finished the cartons of orange juice and *everything*!"

"I know. I thought about that."

"Can we drink sea water?" asked Haley.

"Absolutely not," I told her. "It's full of salt.

131

But we can collect rainwater. Look outside. There's going to be another storm."

"What will we collect it in?" asked Becca sensibly.

"Can you really drink rainwater?" asked Haley.

"Of course you can drink it. And you can collect it in, um, in . . ."

"We'll rig up something," Jeff said.

"Oh, wait a sec. We aren't thinking!" exclaimed Haley. "We can drink coconut milk! I've seen that in lots of films. All you do is climb the coconut tree, pick the coconut, punch holes in the end, and there you go. Coconut milk to drink. I think that would be better than rainwater."

I glanced at Jeff, who shrugged. Finally I said, "Haley, this—this isn't a desert island. There are no coconuts in Connecticut. I promise you."

"But there might be coconut trees on *this* island. We don't know where we are. Can Becca and I please, please, please go and get some coconuts?"

"Well . . . all right. But don't go far. Try to keep the cave in sight. And don't go near the water. And for heaven's sake come back if you get too cold. We don't want any other patients on our hands."

"Okay!" The girls ran off excitedly.

Jeff and I grinned at each other.

"Well, *I'm* going fishing," said Jeff. "I'll try to catch a lot of fish. You know Becca and Haley won't find any coconuts, and they might just be hungry enough to eat some fish."

"Even *I* might eat fish," I said, my stomach rumbling. "As long as I don't have to look at them first."

"I'll cover their heads," said Jeff as he set off.

The cave was quiet for the next hour. Dawn and Jamie slept. I got bored. Very bored. And worried. How *were* we going to get rescued? And where were we? How far could we have drifted? Were we off the coast of Massachusetts now? Or New York? Or were we far out to sea? I had no idea which way the storm had blown us. If only the weather would clear. That would help the search *and* us. On the other hand, we needed the rain for drinking water.

Rain! I'd better think of some way of collecting it.

Now what would hold water? I looked over our few possessions. Only the plastic tarpaulins seemed like good possibilities. But they were flat. We needed a container. And then I had an idea. (I felt like Kristy, who's always getting good ideas.) I left the cave, found four sturdy sticks, stuck them in the sand in front of the cave, and tied one corner of a tarpaulin to each stick. The tarpaulin sagged nicely in the middle. It would hold plenty of water.

I was quite pleased with myself, since I'm not noted for my problem-solving abilities.

When I got back to the cave, Dawn was awake. "What's going on?" she asked, sitting up.

I told her about my rain-catching idea, and that Jeff was out fishing and the girls were out looking for coconuts.

Dawn smiled. Then she leaned over, peered at Jamie, and felt his forehead. "Well, he seems better," she said.

"I know."

At that moment, we heard the patter of rain outside the cave. In moments, Becca, Haley, and Jeff all reappeared. They were wet and chilly, and the girls, of course, had not found any coconuts. But Jeff was carrying quite a few fish.

"Good job!" I said to him. Then I added cheerfully, "Is everyone ready for a fish fry this morning?"

The girls looked dubious. "Are *you* going to eat fish?" Becca asked me.

"Yes I am. As long as I don't have to look— Jeff, keep those things away from me!" I cried as Jeff teased me with the fish.

Jeff and Dawn prepared the fish, and I looked out of the cave entrance at my water collector. "It's working!" I announced. "We'll have water —as long as the tarpaulin doesn't get too full and the sticks collapse."

A little while later, every one of us except Jamie sat down to a breakfast of fish. The girls picked at it at first, but soon they were eating hungrily. I was, too.

"You know," said Becca, "this isn't so bad. It tastes a bit like . . ."

"Chicken?" suggested Haley.

"No. I suppose it just tastes like fish."

"Well, when you're *really* hungry, anything will do," I said.

"Even rattlesnake meat?" asked Jeff.

"No, I'd draw the line there."

"Insects?" asked Becca.

"No!" I cried. I was glad to see everyone laughing, though. We were more likely to pull through this thing if we kept our spirits up.

By the time breakfast was over, the sun was peeping through the clouds, and Jeff, Becca, and Haley ventured outside again. When they had gone, Dawn and I looked at each other. Dawn was frowning.

"What's wrong?" I asked her.

"The children may be in a good mood," she said, "but you do realise that we're in a critical situation, don't you? I mean, we can't live on fish and rainwater forever. And Jamie needs a doctor."

"I know," I said. I let out a breath I didn't even know I'd been holding.

"How far from Stoneybrook do you think we are?"

"I just don't have any idea. And," I went on,

135

anticipating her next question, "I don't know if they're still searching for us. They probably think we've all drowned."

"Claudia!"

"Well, they probably do. But that shouldn't stop us from trying to be rescued. There must be some way to attract attention to ourselves."

"A fire?"

"Too dangerous."

"We could still try to escape. We could build a raft."

"No we couldn't," I said.

"Got any better ideas?"

"No."

"Well, then, we'll just have to keep thinking."

17th CHAPTER

Stacey

Monday

Dear Dad,

Im writing this letter on the train, so I hope you can read my wobbly handwriting. Im really sorry about our fight. I want you to know that Im not angry with you. And I want to come back to New York again soon.

I liked the play on Saturday a lot. But I have to tell you something. Im upset that you didnt let me come home when I needed to. Also I think it is unfair that you and Mum fight over me sometimes. Im sorry you got divorced, but don't put me in the middle. It isn't any easier being a divorced kid than being a divorced parent. My time should be my time, not yours or Mum's.

137

> Thank you for letting me come home early today, and I'll see you in two weeks. I'll phone you as soon as I know what has happened to Dawn and Claud.
>
> LUV,
> Your daughter, Stacey

That was a really difficult letter to write. I felt as if I were telling my father off, and that's something children aren't supposed to do. At least, it was something *this* child isn't supposed to do. I hoped I'd said enough nice things in the letter to make up for the not-so-nice things.

I was supposed to stay in New York until five o'clock on Monday afternoon, but when I woke up on Monday morning, I knew I couldn't stand it there a second longer. I *had* to get back to Stoneybrook and help search for my friends. I knew they hadn't been found yet because I'd spoken to Kristy on Sunday and I'd said, "If they're found, call me straight away, no matter what time it is."

"Even if it's two o'clock in the morning?" Kristy had asked.

"Even then. I don't care if the phone *does* wake my father up."

"We-ell . . ." said Kristy.

138

"*Please*. Promise me."

I knew Kristy would keep a promise. And she hadn't called me. Also, I hadn't seen anything about a rescue on the news.

That does it, I thought, when I woke up at seven-thirty on Monday. I'm going home as soon as I can. No matter what Dad says.

Well, of course, Dad didn't like the idea a bit. That was when we had our fight. Dad watched me throwing stuff into my suitcase and he said, "This was supposed to be a three-day weekend, Stacey."

"Oh, and my friends were *supposed* to get lost at sea on this three-day weekend? It's not as though they *chose* to get lost just to mess up your weekend with me."

"Anastasia!"

"Dad, you're not being fair. If two of your friends were lost—one of them your *best* friend— wouldn't you want to search for them? Or would you just say, 'Hey, it's the weekend. Don't ruin it.'"

"Young lady—" Dad began. Then he stopped. "You really want to leave?"

"*Yes*. I want to get back to Stoneybrook and help search. Everyone else is helping. I feel like a spoiled brat here in the city, going to plays and eating in restaurants. My friends are—well, who knows what they're doing? I bet they aren't having fun or eating good food, though."

Dad shrugged. "If you want to go, go."

139

So I did. I finished packing my suitcase, got into a taxi, and rode to the station. But I felt horrible. I think I'd wanted Dad to say he was sorry. But he hadn't. I was just leaving him all hurt and everything. Of course, I hadn't apologised to him.

So I'd written that letter to Dad. I hoped it would help us to make up. As soon as I'd finished the letter, I tucked it into my rucksack to post later, and tried to forget about New York.

It was time to concentrate on Stoneybrook.

Not much happened during the rest of the journey. I tried to read, but couldn't. I found myself urging the train along instead. Hurry *up*, hurry *up*, hurry *up*, I said in my head to the rhythm of the wheels flying down the tracks.

At last, the train pulled into the Stoneybrook station. I was already standing by the door with my rucksack and my suitcase ready to get off. And that was when I realised something. I hadn't rung Mum from New York. She was expecting me around dinnertime that evening.

"Bother!" I said, as I stepped on to the platform. This was what I got for fighting with Dad and—

"Stacey?"

"Mum?" I couldn't believe it! "How did you know I was on this train?" I asked her.

"Your father called me just after you left the flat."

140

"Oh. So I suppose you know about our fight."

"I know your father's side of it. Come on," said Mum, putting her arm around me and taking the rucksack, which I was struggling with. "Why don't you tell me your side on the way home?"

"Can I tell it to you on the way to the community centre?" I replied. "I want to go straight there and help search."

"Of course," said Mum. So I told her the story as we drove through town.

"I wrote him a letter," I added, as we arrived at the centre.

Mum parked the car, but neither of us got out.

"Do you want to tell me about the letter?" asked my mother.

"I'll do better than that," I said. "You can read it." I searched through my rucksack for the book I'd stuck the letter in. "Here it is." I handed it to Mum. Mum read it and sighed.

"What? Are you angry with me, too?" I asked.

"No," said Mum, but she bent her head over and rested it on her fingertips like she does sometimes when she's angry.

"You are! You *are* angry!" I exclaimed.

And some stupid TV reporter chose *that moment* to stick her microphone through the car window and ask, "Friends of the missing?"

I was stunned. Since I'd been away for the weekend, I had no idea what was going on at the community centre. Now I looked round. The car park was overflowing. Mum wasn't even parked in an actual space, because there weren't any. She'd just pulled up near the door to the centre. I saw a couple of TV vans, a helicopter hovering over the beach near the dock, and a lot of boats.

"What?" I said, searching the face of the reporter. "Are we friends of the missing?"

"Yes," said the reporter.

"I am," I replied.

"Well, how do you *feel*, knowing that your friends are gone?"

"I feel terrible!" I cried. "What did you expect? I feel—"

Mum cut me short. She put an end to the interview by pressing the button that closes all the windows in the car. The reporter had to act quickly to get her microphone out before it got squashed by the window.

"Mum!" I exclaimed. Then I paused. "Thanks," I said.

We both began to laugh.

"Darling," said my mother, "I'm not angry. Really I'm not. At least not with you. I think I'm angry with myself, though. And maybe with your father. We don't mean to put you in the middle of things, but if we do . . . then we should stop. I promise we'll try harder."

"Thanks," I said. I looked out of the window. "Gosh! I wonder what's going on." There was a

142

flurry of activity among the news reporters. They were all running towards the centre. "Maybe there's some news!" I exclaimed. "Come on, Mum!"

We dashed inside, even though our car wasn't properly parked. And the first person I saw in that crowded room was Kristy.

"Stacey!" she cried.

"Kristy!"

We hugged quickly.

Then I said, "What happened? What's going on?" at the same time as *Kristy* said, "You're home early!"

"I know. I'll explain later," I told her. "But what *is* this?"

Kristy sighed. "I don't know what to make of this news, but one of the search boats found an empty sailing boat early this morning. It's Claudia's. They checked the numbers on the boat. There's no question about it. The boat is in good condition, but it's completely empty. I mean, even the food and supplies are missing."

"An empty boat," I repeated slowly.

Kristy nodded.

"No hole or anything?"

"No. It was just floating along."

At that point we heard a reporter saying to a tired-looking searcher, "You say there were no signs of a struggle on board?"

"A *struggle*?" said Kristy. "What do they think

143

happened? That pirates raided the sailing boat?" Kristy looked furious.

"Never mind," I said to her.

"Hey, you two!"

Mallory ran up to us then.

"We heard the news," said Kristy before Mallory could go on.

"Well, what are we waiting for?" said Mal. "Mum and Dad and the triplets and Nicky and Vanessa are here. We're ready to go searching again. Who wants to come with us?"

I don't know why, exactly, but some reason, instead of answering Mal, I burst into tears.

"Stacey?" said my mother from behind me.

"They found one of the sailing boats this morning," I said hysterically. "It was empty. That can't be a good sign!"

"Oh, Stace," said Mum. "Come on. Let's go home."

I almost went with her. But at the last moment I turned round. "Wait," I said. "I want to search after all. That's why I came home, isn't it? To search?"

"How many times have you been out on a boat?" Mum wanted to know. "Other than a cruise ship."

"Almost none. But I *have* to go. And Mal says they've got room for me."

"We-ell . . ."

Mum had softened. "See you later!" I called to her.

I ran back to Kristy and Mallory and the rest of the Pikes. "Is there still room for me?" I asked.

"Of course," said Mrs Pike. "Okay, everybody. Let's get ready."

18th CHAPTER

Mallory

Monday

My diary has certainly become full the last few days. I'm sorry that it had to become full because of a tragedy but, in a way, I like having a record of the mystery and the search. I wonder if that's morbid. No. I have a feeling that one day this will be useful or meaningful to someone.

Today we went looking for our lost friends again. We've spent so much time on the water that whenever I close my eyes now, all I see is an endless blue-green expanse. And I can feel the boat rocking under me. At least today's search was different from yesterday's. I don't know if it was better, though. Just different. What made it different was that on today's search, we actually found something....

146

Monday morning started early, unlike most holidays. By seven o'clock, I could hear Mum and Dad rustling around in the kitchen. Even though they'd said the night before that we wouldn't go out on any boats today until late in the morning or even lunchtime, I joined them for an early breakfast. I like spending quiet time alone with Mum and Dad.

But by eleven-thirty that morning my family, except for Claire and Margo, who stayed behind with Mary Anne, had gathered at the community centre, ready for another day of boating and searching. We met Kristy and Stacey at the centre. They wanted to come with us, especially since there was finally some news: Claudia's boat had been found. It was in perfect condition—but empty.

"I don't get it," I said to Dad. "What could that mean?"

Dad was frowning. "I don't know. That's a real mystery."

"The food and supplies have gone," I said thoughtfully. "Maybe it's a good sign. How could those things just disappear from the boat? They must have been taken off. Some of them are stored under the seats."

"That's a good point," said Dad.

The reporters, of course, were terribly excited by the news. They picked it up and shook it like a dog with a rabbit, and wouldn't let it go.

Mallory
i

They drove everyone round the bend.

Dad wanted to get us organised and on boats again. He called all of us—our family, Kristy, and Stacey—together on the quay behind the centre.

"Since there are so many of us, we'll take two big boats out today. We'll divide up like this: Kristy, Stacey, Mal and Jordan with me. The rest of you with your mum."

Of course, Kristy and Stacey and I liked this arrangement. We *wanted* to be together. Unfortunately, so did the triplets—Jordan, Adam, and Byron. They didn't want to be split up, but they didn't have a say in the matter.

"Life jackets, everyone," announced Dad.

We separated, stepped on to the boats, and put on life jackets.

Our second day of searching had begun.

We left the quay behind us and headed into Long Island Sound.

"Which way are we going?" I asked Dad. "Back to Greenpoint again?"

"I think we'll go east of there," he replied. "The empty boat was found several miles to the east."

"Okay."

Dad steered the boat, and Stacey, Kristy, and Jordan and I hung over the sides, looking, looking, looking.

"What are we looking *for*?" asked Stacey.

"Anything unusual," said Dad.

148

"Hey!" said Jordan. "I've got an idea. Let's bear east but let's go there by way of all the little islands. We can go out to Greenpoint and then go east. That way, if they landed on one of the islands, we can see them and rescue them."

(Jordan desperately wanted to be a hero.)

"Well," said Dad, "okay. That'll take a long time to do, but it's a good idea."

I imagined us passing an island and hearing cries.

"Help! Here we are! Rescue us!"

Hmmm. Maybe it would be fun to be heroes.

So we headed towards Greenpoint and soon passed it. We didn't talk much as we moved. We just looked and looked and looked at the water and the islands. The water was as smooth as glass, and the colour of an emerald. But the sky was still hazy and . . . .

"Look up there," said Kristy.

"What? What can you see?" asked Stacey, swivelling round.

"Oh, sorry," replied Kristy. "I can't see *them*. It's just, well, I think we're in for another storm."

Kristy was pointing to clouds, to looming thunderheads.

"Oh no!" murmured Jordan.

"How much time do we have?" I asked Dad. "When do we have to turn round?"

"Now," my father answered. "We don't want to get caught in that storm."

"Why can't the weather clear up?" I cried. I nearly stamped my foot. I was so frustrated. "We'll never find anything this way. Not if we have to keep turning the boat round and coming in."

Nobody answered me. They knew the weather was something we just had to put up with.

"Uh-oh!" said Stacey suddenly. "Mr Pike, what if Mrs Pike didn't see the storm clouds? What if they aren't coming in?"

"They're coming," my dad answered. "I just spoke to Adam on the radio."

"Where are they, anyway?" wondered Stacey. "I lost sight of them."

"They're a little ahead of us, but not this far east," said Jordan. "Right, Dad?"

"Exactly right."

We had turned round and were heading back. Jordan and my friends and I continued to scan the water for . . . anything.

We were about half-way back to Stoneybrook when Stacey said, "What's that?"

"What's what?" replied Jordan, who was standing next to her.

"That." Stacey point out to sea. "Over there."

Stacey must have eyes like an eagle to see through the haze. I couldn't see anything but water.

"Mr Pike," said Stacey, "I can see something

150

floating over there. Honestly. Can we get a bit closer to it?"

Dad looked at the sky and then at his watch. "Okay," he said. "Here we go."

We headed east slightly. Soon even I could see something in the water. But we weren't sure what it was until we were practically on top of it.

"A piece of wood," said Kristy.

"Hey, there's another one!" shouted Jordan, pointing.

"Can you see any numbers or letters on it?" asked Dad.

"Yes," said Stacey straight away, not knowing what my father was getting at. "I can see a two, a three, and maybe part of a five.

Dad looked grim.

"It's from Dawn's boat, isn't it?" I said. My voice had dropped to a whisper.

"From Dawn's boat?" repeated Stace. "What do you mean?"

"We know what to look for," said Dad gently. "The numbers on the boats are what identify them."

"And the number on Dawn's boat had a two-three-five in it?" asked Stacey.

"Yes," replied Dad.

"But . . . it can't—I mean, that boat is in pieces. It's completely broken up. I can see lots of others . . ." Stacey trailed off.

151

Dad put us back on course to Stoneybrook
again.

"Wait!" cried Stacey. "We can't turn round
now."

"We've got to," said Kristy, who'd been
awfully quiet. "We've got to beat the storm back.
And we've got to report what we found. Don't
worry, th—"

Stacey cut her off. Just barely holding back
tears, she cried, "Don't worry? You're as bad as
my father. Claudia and the others are . . . well,
who knows where they are? Obviously, they're
not on either of the boats. And think of all the
stuff that's out here waiting to get them! There
could be sharks, sea snakes, jellyfish. Not to
mention these storms we keep having."

Kristy put her arm round Stacey. I wanted to
do the same thing, since Stacey had started to cry.
But then I started to cry, too.

Jordan didn't know what to make of the
situation. He was as startled by the discovery of
the bits of boat as we were, and he was worried
about Jeff, who's his friend, but he gave my father
a look that plainly said, "*Girls!*"

Dad didn't notice. Yelling over the wind that
was starting to pick up, he said, "I really don't
think you need to worry about sharks or sea
snakes, girls. Trust me."

"Okay, what about drowning?" Stacey yelled
back.

152

No one had an answer for that.

We sailed back to the community centre in silence, unless you count the blustery wind that roared in our ears. We reached the centre just after Mum and the others—and just as it started to rain. The boats were barely docked when fat raindrops started falling from the sky, and thunder rumbled. We dashed into the centre, where Dad made a report about what we'd found.

Naturally, the reporters went wild, especially when they noticed that Kristy, Stacey, and I were all in tears.

We were rescued from their questions, though. Both Mrs McGill and Charlie Thomas were at the centre, so they drove Stacey and Kristy to their homes. Then my family and I went back to our house, where Mum actually put me to bed and made me some tea. I can't remember the last time I've been so upset.

Soon, though, feeling better, I phoned Stacey. We talked about everything except the awful pieces of wood.

"Do you think school will be open tomorrow?" Stacey wondered.

"I don't know," I replied. "Everyone's searching. Half the teachers from SMS have been combing the beach."

When Stacey and I had rung off, I just sat on Mum and Dad's bed. I didn't know what to do.

I felt completely helpless.

19th CHAPTER

Claudia

Looking Back-
Late Mondy Mornig and
Early Mondy Afternon

I was sick and tried of of all those long faces everyone was just mopping around and it was making me crazy. I decided to do somthing about it. So I left dawn watching jamie and I left Jeff watching the girls and I went into the woods to see what I could find....

My water collection idea had worked pretty well, but just after breakfast we discovered something: you couldn't leave it alone too long, especially if the rain was coming down hard.

Becca and Haley were tidying up after our breakfast, which meant collecting up the fish bones and putting them outside the cave. (We decided that they were organic refuse and would disintegrate, unlike the rest of our rubbish.)

"Besides," said Becca, working hastily, "we don't want the cave to smell of fish." Then she added, "Not that the fish was bad, Jeff."

Jeff grinned. He knew that Becca and Haley and I had eaten the fish out of desperation, but he didn't mind.

Becca had just run out of the cave with her pile of fish bones when the rest of us heard her exclaim, "Uh-oh!"

"What-oh?" asked Haley.

"Everybody get out here quickly!" cried Becca.

Jeff and Haley and I joined her, but Dawn stayed behind with Jamie. Nobody had to ask Becca what the problem was. We could see it clearly. The water collector was full and about to collapse.

"Quick! Everyone hold tight to the posts. Don't let them cave in!" I yelled. Then I dashed inside and gathered up every empty container I could find. When I ran back out, I saw Jeff,

Haley, and Becca each straining to hold up a stick. The fourth pole was about to cave in.

As quickly as I could, I submerged each bottle in the water, filled it to the brim, and put it on the ground. I had almost finished when . . . *whoosh, crash*! That fourth pole collapsed and the rest of the water splashed to the ground.

"Bother!" cried Jeff. "All that wasted water."

"Well, it could be worse," said Haley philosophically. "At least we've got *some* water. And there'll probably be another storm soon. Then we can collect more."

"That's true," I said. "Come on, you lot. Help me set everything up again. We might as well be prepared."

The children and I put the poles back and tied the tarpaulin to them again. Then we examined our water supply.

"I suppose it's not the most hygienic in the world," I said, thinking that everyone had taken a drink from every bottle and that the water hadn't been purified, and I wasn't sure how clean the tarpaulin had been. "But it's better than nothing."

"It certainly is," agreed Haley. She picked up an orange juice carton that we'd torn open, and drank thirstily. "Not bad," she remarked, after she'd drunk half of it.

"Okay, slow down everybody," I warned them. "Jamie will need some of this water, and we should make the rest of it last as long as we can."

156

The children helped me bring the water into the cave. I carried a bottle over to Jamie. "How's he doing?" I asked Dawn.

Dawn's face was as long as—as I'm not sure what. She looked awful.

"Not very well," she replied. "I think his temperature's up again. And I've been wondering. Do you think we should wake him up to feed him?"

"Feed him *fish*?" I said, horrified. "He'd never forgive us."

"I'm serious. He hasn't eaten since lunch yesterday, and that was just a chocolate bar. He probably needs food to help him fight whatever he's got."

"I don't know. I wouldn't wake him up just to feed him. But if he wakes up on his own and says he's hungry, then Jeff can go fishing again. Meanwhile, here's some more water."

"Oh, good," said Dawn. "I *am* going to wake him up for a drink. His temperature was down as long as he kept having water."

So Dawn and I roused the sleeping Jamie.

"We've got more water," Dawn told him.

I helped her raise Jamie into a sitting position. Jamie drank for a long time. Then he fell asleep again.

"Claudia, can we go to the beach?" asked Haley, not looking terribly enthusiastic about the

157

idea. "All of us?" Then she added dramatically, "The air is thick with germs."

"Of course. I'll come with you. Or perhaps Dawn will." I turned to Dawn. "Do you want to take a break and go to the beach?"

Dawn shook her head. "I'll stay here with the germs." She was trying to be funny, but she looked as though she was going to cry at any second.

"All right," I said hesitantly.

I walked outside with the children. Their faces now looked about as long as Dawn's. I was pretty sure that now that the excitement of breakfast and water-collecting was over, they were starting to worry again. And they were bored with the beach. That much was obvious.

We reached the edge of the water and the children plopped down and just sat there. They didn't even talk. After a few minutes I couldn't take it any more. I had to *do* something.

"All right," I said, "I'm going for a little walk. Jeff, you're in charge. Dawn's in the cave if you have any problems. Stay out of the water and don't go anywhere without telling Dawn." Before they could ask questions, I took off. I marched into the woods.

How, I wondered, could we attract attention to ourselves so that we could be rescued? Becca had been right in trying to attract the attention of the searchplanes, but the shells weren't going to work. What else could be seen from a plane? I looked all around me. I saw trees and shrubs and some flowers I didn't recognize. I saw poison ivy and avoided it. I noticed logs and leaves and branches and insects.

And then I saw something bright on the ground. What was it? I bent down and picked up a broken piece of . . . glass? No, I could see myself in it. It was a piece of mirror. It was big, and the edges were jagged. I had to hold it carefully. I didn't know how it had found its way to the island, but I knew what to do with it.

I raced out of the woods, along the beach to the cave, and inside the cave to Dawn, who was dozing next to Jamie.

I shook her shoulder. "Look what I've found!" I said in an excited whisper.

"What?" Dawn sat up sleepily.

"A mirror, that's what."

"Big deal! And where have you been? I looked outside earlier on and I couldn't see you. Just Jeff and Becca and Haley."

Ooh, touchy! I ignored Dawn's outburst. "Don't you know what we can do with this?" I asked her. "If we wash it clean, we can use it to signal to planes. Seriously. *I* saw it from above because it was lying in a little patch of sunlight. If I saw it, maybe a plane could see it—if the haze ever disperses. We just have to learn how to angle it to catch the sun. I think."

"We-ell," said Dawn dubiously.

"Look, we haven't got any better ideas," I told her. "And it will give the children something to do, um, as soon as this next storm blows over."

I'd just noticed how dark the sky was, so I herded Haley, Becca, and Jeff back inside. We waited for the brief shower to finish, filled empty containers, and cheered because the water collector didn't collapse.

And then . . . and then . . . we noticed something. The sky had become as clear as a bell! We ran to the beach with our prize, the mirror.

"I want to wash it!" cried Haley, dashing to the sea.

"Okay, but be careful. It's sharp," I warned.

Haley washed the mirror as if she was washing a bomb. Then she dried it on her shirt and handed it to me.

"Beautiful," I told her. I looked at the sky. "Now let's hope the sun stays out."

"And that a plane flies overhead," Jeff pointed out.

That was true. In the meantime, we experimented. The sun did stay out and the four of us stood on the beach and practised trying to catch its rays.

Once, Becca did, and she nearly blinded us with the glare.

"It's a bit like calling Batman!" she exclaimed.

We laughed.

I was glad that the children seemed hopeful again, but I knew that what we were trying to do had only a slim chance of working. We hadn't seen a plane all day.

Still, you never knew.

"Come and save us, Batman!" cried Haley.

20th CHAPTER

Kristy

Sunday Morning's
Emergency Meeting
(continued)

Bart was not at all pleased when I
phoned to tell him that I was cancelling
Monday's game. He just didn't understand.
He felt bad about the boating accident
but, he wondered, what I could do.
Before I could answer his question, he
rushed ahead. He said... Well, he said
some pretty nasty things. But they don't
belong in notes of an emergency
meeting.

162

When I picked up the phone that Sunday to call Bart, I was half hoping he wouldn't be there. Unfortunately, Bart himself answered the phone.

"Hello?" he said.

I knew it was Bart's voice. "Hi!" I replied. "It's me, Kristy."

I was using the Pikes' upstairs phone and hoped no one was listening to my call.

"Hi!" Bart sounded glad to hear from me. That would wear off soon. "What's the matter?" he asked. Then he rushed on, "Oh, any news of your friends?"

"No. That's why I'm calling. Bart, I want to go out searching with the Pikes today, which means I won't be able to take the practice for the Krushers. Besides, half the children on the team are either searching or down at the community centre waiting for news, so they couldn't come anyway. I've got to call off our game tomorrow. We can't hold it if we don't practise." What I didn't add was that if my friends hadn't been found by tomorrow then we'd probably go out searching again anyway. But I didn't want to think about that.

There was silence at Bart's end of the phone.

"Bart?" I said.

"Yes?"

"Did you hear me?"

"I heard you."

"So our game's off. I'm sorry. We'll have to reschedule it."

"Kristy, I think this is pretty irresponsible of you. We've had the game arranged for weeks. You're going to disappoint a lot of people."

I was stunned by the word "irresponsible". I cleared my throat. "Excuse me! Did you say I'm being irresponsible? Because I want to help search for six missing people, two of whom are very close friends of mine, one of whom is a Krusher, and another of whom is a Krusher cheerleader? I'm a bit confused. I don't understand the 'irresponsibility' part."

"Don't be sarcastic, Kristy."

"Me? Sarcastic?"

"Look, I know your team probably isn't ready for the game tomorrow, but that's no reason to cancel it."

"Is that what you think I'm trying to do? Worm my way out of the game?"

"Well—"

"Come on. Tell me. I can take it."

"Okay. Yes, that's what I think you're doing. Your team hasn't beaten mine yet. I think you just don't want to see the Krushers disappointed ag—"

Bart got cut off when I put the phone down on him.

That was Sunday morning. By early Monday afternoon I hadn't heard from him, although I suppose I hadn't really expected to. I mean, I had put the phone down on him. Maybe that was childish, but Bart was being pretty childish himself. What was wrong with him? Hadn't he ever had an emergency before?

On top of that, didn't he realise that he was making a miserable weekend even more miserable? How dare he pick a fight with me when six people I liked a lot were *missing*?

I soon found that after that awful phone call, Bart was always on my mind. Or at least at the back of my mind. He was there when the Pikes and I went out searching on Sunday afternoon. He was there all evening as I watched the stupid TV coverage of the *Connecticut Disaster*, waiting for news that didn't come. He was there the next day when the empty boat was discovered, and later when Stacey spotted the pieces of what was probably Dawn's boat.

As Charlie drove me home from the centre on Monday, I wondered if I would ever speak to Bart again. Would the Krushers ever play Bart's Bashers again, or had I ruined everything?

I had no idea, and no extra energy to try to work it out.

While Charlie was parking the car at our house, I ran inside, crying. I still couldn't get over the fact that we'd found the wreckage of one of the boats.

"Kristy?" said Mum. She was surprised to see me in tears. "What's the matter?" She paused. Then she put her hand to her mouth. "Oh, no!"

she whispered. "It's bad news, isn't it?"

"No," I said quickly, brushing away my tears. "It isn't that. But Stacey found pieces of Dawn's boat."

"Are you sure it was Dawn's boat?" asked Watson, my stepfather. The three of us sat down in the living room. Soon Charlie joined us.

"Well, pretty sure," I answered. "Stacey saw numbers on one piece of wood, and they were three of the numbers on Dawn's boat. In the right order," I added.

"But not the whole number?" said Watson.

"Noooo," I replied slowly.

"Then you can't be sure it was Dawn's boat," Watson pointed out sensibly.

"That's true." I felt just a tiny bit better. Then Bart crept into my mind and I felt awful again.

At that moment the phone rang. I know this is awful, but my first thought was, I hope it's Bart. That was stupid, though. Things hardly ever work out the way you think they will.

"I'll get it!" I cried anyway. I jumped up.

Watson put his hand out. "Resume yourself," he said, which means, "Sit down." He smiled. "Karen's getting it, I'm sure." (Karen and Andrew were spending the long weekend with us.) "Karen can't get enough of the phone these days."

I listened, but the phone didn't ring again. A few seconds later, Karen bounced into the living room, calling, "Are you here, Kristy?"

"Is it for me?" I got to my feet.

"Mm-hmm." Karen was grinning.

"Why are you smiling?"

"Because . . ." (Karen ran to me, and tugged at me. I leaned over.) "It's your boyfriend! You told me not to say that any more," she added.

So it *was* Bart after all!

I flew to the extension in Mum and Watson's bedroom, which is the most private extension, calling for Karen to hang up in the kitchen.

"Bart?" I said breathlessly.

"Hi, Kristy." Bart sounded funny. A bit depressed or somehing.

"Are you okay?" I asked.

"Yes. It's just that I've been watching TV for hours now and I feel terrible about our conversation yesterday. I suppose, um, I suppose I want to apologise. I mean, I *do* want to apologise. I'm sorry."

"That's okay. I'm sorry I hung up on you."

"That's okay."

There was a silence. Finally Bart said, "Maybe this isn't the right time to tell you this, so stop me if you don't want to hear it, but I really feel I must say something."

"Okay." Oh, no! What was he going to say? Was he dumping me?

"The thing is," Bart began, "you exaggerate sometimes."

I burst out laughing. "No, really?" Then I

added, "Sorry. It's just that I know I've got a big mouth. I'm always getting in trouble because of it."

"Okay. But, you see, I can't always tell when you're being straightforward and when you're exaggerating. It would help me a lot if—"

"I won't cry wolf any more," I told him. "That's a promise."

"Thank you." Bart sounded as relieved as I felt. Then he said, "Listen, I want to help search, if there's anything I can do. And once your friends are found—and I know they will be—*then* we'll talk about rescheduling our game. Is that okay with you?"

Was it okay with me? Of course. In fact, it was great!

"Do you want to go to the community centre—?"

Bart was interrupted by some strange clicks on the phone. At first I thought Karen was eavesdropping on us. I was about to let her have it, when a voice came on the line:

"This is the operator. Is Kristy Thomas there? I have an emergency call for her from a Jessi Ramsey."

"This is Kristy!" I said excitedly. Wow! I'd never had an *emergency* call before.

"Kristy," said the operator, "please ask your caller to ring off so that you can talk to Jessi."

"Okay," I replied. "Bart?"

"I'll talk to you later," he said instantly. He hung up.

And then Jessi was on the line. "Kristy! Kristy! I can't talk long, but the community centre just rang to say that they've been found. All of them. And they're alive! They're on a little island further up the coast."

I couldn't believe it. I was afraid to believe it. But that didn't prevent me from spreading the news to everyone I could think of.

21st CHAPTER

Claudia

Looking Back —
Monday Afternoon

The miror worked! It relly did!
How many grate ideas can I get?
Frist the water colecter and now the
plane singal. Mabe I should become
an inventor insted of a artist I
would probably make more money.

Anyway it was relly funny the
kids were calling for batmen. They
were just playing arond yelling, Come and
get us batman! Here we are! And
here is are bat singal! Please come and
reskew us.

And out of nowhere help arrived....

"Batman! Here we are, Batman!" yelled Becca.

"Yes, here's our bat signal!" shouted Haley, aiming the mirror expertly at the sun.

"Hey! What's that?" exclaimed Jeff. "Be quiet, you lot," he said impatiently to Haley and Becca.

"What is it?" I asked him.

"SHHH," hissed Jeff. "Just listen."

The four of us stopped and listened.

And we heard a plane.

"An aeroplane, an aeroplane! Oh, my lord, an aeroplane!" I shrieked.

"Where is it?" asked Haley.

The four of us craned our necks back. Haley was still holding the mirror.

"There it is!" I cried. "Haley, aim the mirror! Aim it at the plane."

"I'll do it!" said Jeff.

"No, I will!" We were all grabbing for the mirror.

"Well, *somebody* do it—quick!" shouted Becca. She was jumping up and down, waving her arms frantically.

In the end, I was the one who held the mirror and aimed. "I just hope they can see that," I muttered.

And they could! The plane continued to fly straight ahead. Then slowly it circled back over the island and flew lower . . . and lower. It dipped its wings.

Jeff, Haley, Becca, and I were screaming and

171

running around. We stopped when the plane dipped its wings, though. We'd never seen a plane do that.

Then we heard a voice from the sky. "This is a search plane!"

"Aagghhh! It *is* Batman!" shrieked Becca.

"Shh! No, it isn't," I told her.

"Wave your arms if you are Claudia or Dawn." The voice was deep. It was coming over a loud hailer.

I waved my arms.

"Wave again to let us know if you are all on the island."

I waved.

"And wave again if you need a doctor."

I waved.

"Okay. We'll send a Coastguard ship to you as fast as we can. It will come equipped with food, water, a doctor, and your parents."

"And some Hula Hoops!" I yelled back, but I'm sure the pilot (or whoever was yelling) couldn't hear me.

Another dip of the wings, and the plane headed off in the direction from which it had come.

"We're saved! Oh, my lord, we're saved!" I cried.

"At last," said Jeff.

"Yes, it took them long enough," added Haley.

We looked at her and began to laugh.

172

"Come on. We've got to tell Dawn," I said. "We'll have to get Jamie ready to go, and put out our fire, and you lot make sure we've got all our things with us. I don't want anyone getting home and complaining, 'Claudia, I left my T-shirt on the island'."

We ran back to the cave in high spirits.

"Dawn! Dawn! The mirror worked!" Becca cried as soon as we reached the cave entrance. "A plane flew over and a man's sending a boat and our parents will be on it!"

"Stop teasing! said Dawn sulkily.

"She isn't teasing," I said. "It just happened. Didn't you hear the man with the loudhailer?"

"No," replied Dawn. Then she added, "You aren't teasing, are you? That would be much too unkind."

"It's the truth. Batman's honour," Jeff told his sister.

Dawn jumped up then and hugged first her brother, then me. And soon we were all hugging, except for Jamie. But a few minutes later, he woke up; groggily, though.

"What are you doing?" he mumbled.

"Celebrating!" replied Dawn. "We're going to be rescued. A plane saw us and a ship will be on its way. Your mummy and daddy will be on the ship."

"A doctor, too," I added. "I'm sure he—"

"Or she—" chimed in Haley.

"—will help you to start feeling better straight away."

"Goody!" said Jamie, and he fell asleep again.

The wait for the Coastguard boat seemed endless. Actually, it did take a couple of hours to reach us. But it seemed more like a couple of days. While we were waiting, we gathered up our belongings. (That took about five minutes.) We decided, though, not to put out our fire or take down our water collector until the Coastguard ship had actually arrived. We'd learned the hard way that you never know what to expect.

Dawn and I were in the cave watching Jamie, whose breathing sounded a bit strange, and the children were outside near the cave entrance, when Jeff shouted, "I can see it! I think I can see it!"

I was on my feet in a flash. Sure enough, far off in the distance was what looked like a boat. Becca, Haley, Jeff, and I ran to the water's edge and began screaming and waving our arms again. We were afraid the ship would pass us by.

It didn't, though. But since it was huge (well, big) it had to dock offshore. A smaller boat was lowered into the water and a couple of men and a woman were sent to meet us. I guessed that one of them was the doctor.

You know what was the most frustrating thing about our rescue? We could see our parents on the boat—they were all waving and leaning over the side so far that I was afraid they'd fall into the water, or tip the boat over— but they couldn't come to us and we couldn't go to them. At least, not yet. The doctor would probably check Jamie first, and then we'd go out to the ship on lifeboats. All we could do was wave.

When the first lifeboat came ashore, a man in a sailor's uniform stepped out and waded in to meet us. He and the other man were Coastguards. The woman was the doctor.

"See? I told you," hissed Haley. "The doctor's a woman."

We didn't know those three people from a hole in the wall (as Kristy's stepfather would say) but as soon as they were standing on the beach, we hugged them. I even cried a little, but they were happy tears. You know what? The three of *them* cried, too.

One of the men even said, "You don't know how glad we are to see you."

"Wrong," I replied. "You don't know how glad *we* are to see *you*!"

Everyone laughed. Then the woman, whose name was Dr Weber, said briskly, "Now, who needs a doctor? All of you look pretty healthy."

"It's Jamie Newton," I told her. "He's four. He became ill late yesterday afternoon. We're not sure what he's got, but he's running a high temperature. Well, it was higher yesterday before we began forcing him to drink. And he aches all over, his throat's sore, he's got earache, and now his breathing's funny."

"Okay. I'll look at him. He could have a throat infection, or maybe 'flu. Where is he?"

"In our cave, with Dawn," I replied.

"Yes, come on," said Becca. "We'll show you."

We walked up the beach with the doctor and the Coastguards.

"There's our water collector," said Jeff, as we approached the cave. "Claudia invented it. It really works."

"Pretty clever," said one of the men. "So you've had shelter and water for the last couple of days. That's good. What about food?"

"Fish and chocolate bars," Haley told him, looking disgusted. "I hope you've got good food on your boat."

"Plenty," replied the man. "Water and juice, too."

The four of us sighed with relief—and hunger.

We went into the cave then, introduced Dawn to our rescuers, and let the doctor examine Jamie. The doctor looked rather concerned, but managed to get some medicine into him. Then she said, "The sooner we get him to a hospital, the better. Oh," she went on, seeing our stricken faces, "he's not *that* ill, but I need to run a few tests, get his temperature down, and just watch him for a while. He's lucky he had such good care here. You couldn't have done better."

176

Dawn and I smiled.

One of the men picked Jamie up then, Jeff put out our fire with rainwater, we gathered up our rubbish and belongings, and before we knew it, we were standing on the beach, where two more lifeboats had been sent in.

"Goodbye, Nine O'Clock Island," whispered Becca as we were rowed out to the ship.

We were still approaching the ship when the screaming and cheering began.

What a reunion! There have been times when I was so angry with my parents that I wanted to divorce them. But when I finally stepped on to the Coastguard ship, there were no faces I wanted to see more than Mum's and Dad's.

We hugged practically for ever.

And Dawn and Jeff were hugging their mum and stepfather, Becca and Haley were hugging their parents, and Jamie's parents were fussing over him. I think everybody on board that boat was crying.

And eating. We castaways tucked into the food and wolfed it down. While I ate, I tried to tell Mum and Dad about the last 48 hours—how we had ended up on the island and how I, Claudia Kishi, had got us off the island. I told them about the water collector, too.

"You know," I finished, "I *do* promise to study harder at school, but I have to admit, I don't feel nearly so bad about my school report now. I may not be school-clever or book-clever but I'm practical. I think I'm pretty good at solving problems, aren't I?"

Mum's and Dad's answers? More hugs and tears.

I smiled at them. The boat was halfway to Stoneybrook by then. In a little while we would be back with our friends and brothers and sisters. Home sweet home!

22nd CHAPTER

Dawn

*Looking Back—
Monday Afternoon*

Well.

It's hard to describe our homecoming. It was both the happiest and the most emotional time of my life. Even more emotional (for me) than Mum and Richard's wedding. I suppose you just have to have been shipwrecked, washed ashore on an island, and stranded there for two days before you know how it feels to get home and see your family and friends again.

The boat trip to Stoneybrook was pretty incredible, but the reunion at the community centre was amazing. Everyone was there—our brothers and sisters, our friends, and... the reporters.

179

Dawn

My mother could hardly stop hugging Jeff and me as the Coastguard ship sailed us home. It was as if she couldn't believe we were really safe and alive unless she could touch us. She told us how worried she and Richard had been, and that they'd tried all weekend to get in touch with Dad, but hadn't reached him until just after they got the news that we'd been found.

"Mum?" I said at one point when she'd managed to let go of Jeff, who had run off. "I've got to tell you something."

"What is it? This sounds like a confession."

"I suppose it is, sort of."

"Okay."

"Well, the thing is, um, the thing is . . ." Mum was watching me seriously. "The thing is, I wasn't much help on the island. I sort of fell apart. I looked after Jamie, but Claudia was the one who did all the thinking. She worked out how to collect rainwater, instead of going without water. And she worked out how to attract attention to ourselves so that we could be rescued. She really kept things going."

"Darling, everyone reacts differently in an emergency."

"I know, but I feel I let everyone down. Or maybe I just feel I let myself down. I mean, my friends always tell me what a clear head I've got. They say I don't let things get me down. But this *did* get me down. I was just another person for Claudia to take care of."

"I don't know, darling," said Mum. "Maybe you didn't come through quite the way you would have expected, but you did know how to look after Jamie. And I don't think you really fell apart. Suppose the fire in your cave had started burning out of control. Would you have rescued the children?"

"Of course!"

"If somebody had been injured, would you have tried to give them first aid?"

"Yes."

"Okay. Then you didn't fall apart. But maybe you learned something about yourself."

"That I'm a worrier?"

Mum laughed. "No. That you can't always be the strong one. And by not being the strong one for once, I think you helped Claudia learn something about herself."

"That she *can* be the strong one? That she can work out problems?"

"Exactly."

Mum and I hugged. (Again.) I felt much better. Good enough to eat some more of the fruit she'd brought with her.

Not much later I heard a cry: "There it is! There's the quay!"

I turned to look. Sure enough, ahead of us and to our right was the quay and the community

181

centre. I hardly recognised the quay, though. As we drew closer, I saw why. It was so covered with people that from a distance it looked furry.

"Gosh!" I said under my breath.

Soon the ship was docking. First off were the Newtons and Dr Weber.

The crowd cheered.

Then Mum, Richard, Jeff, and I got off.

More cheering.

Where were all the cameras and reporters? I wondered.

Before I had an answer to my question, I spotted Mary Anne. She and Logan were at the front of the crowd. For ages we just stared at each other. Then Mary Anne held out her arms and I ran to her.

"I promise never to fight with you again!" I cried, at the same time as Mary Anne cried, "I'll never stop speaking to you again!"

"Ever?" I asked her. "Even if I forget to give you messages for the rest of my life? Or the rest of your life?"

"Even then."

"Gosh!" I said. "I ought to get shipwrecked more often."

Mary Anne and Logan and I laughed. And Mary Anne turned to Logan and said, "Do you forgive me? I'm *really* sorry I thought you'd stood me up. But what else was I supposed to think? We'd arranged to meet and you weren't there. I hadn't got the message."

"I know, I know, I know," said Logan. "I hope *you'll* forgive me."

"I will," replied Mary Anne.

(Phew! Our rescue was patching up all sorts of arguments.)

I really think Mary Anne and Logan might have kissed right there on the quay but they realised that Mum and Richard were there, not to mention about a million people with cameras.

I turned away. I wanted to watch the rest of the castaways have their reunions. Haley had been right behind me. Now she and her brother, Matt, were holding a frantic, happy, sign-language reunion. Since Haley's hands were busier than Matt's, I had a pretty good idea that she was telling him about the adventure and how we had survived.

Haley and her parents were followed off the ship by Becca and her parents. I watched Becca fly into Jessi's arms. Jessi was with Squirt and some lady I didn't know. The lady looked a little like Mr Ramsey, but I'd never seen her before.

"Becca!" Jessi cried.

"Jessi!" Becca cried.

It was like something out of a film.

"You'll never believe this," Becca said, speaking as fast as she could, "but I *ate fish*! I really did!"

I laughed. Becca spends two days stranded

who-knows-where, and all she can say about her adventure is that she ate fish!

"Hey, Becca," said Jessi, who was laughing, too. "Would you clear something up for me? Would you tell Aunt Cecelia" (Aunt Cecelia?) "who gave you permission to go sailing?"

"Mummy and Daddy did," replied Becca. Then she added, "Aunt Cecelia, why are you here?"

"It's a long story," Jessi answered before her aunt could open her mouth. Then she said, "See? It really wasn't my fault."

"Hmphh," said Aunt Cecelia. But she gave Jessi a half-smile.

Last off the boat were Claudia and her parents. Claud was greeted by her sister, Janine. They hugged uncomfortably, but looked glad to see each other. I bet Claud couldn't wait to tell the Genius about her water collector and the mirror signal.

"Hey! Hey, Dawn!" yelled a voice.

I looked round. I was in the middle of an enormous, noisy crowd. I saw my brother talking to the Pike triplets. I saw some reporters interviewing parents and scribbling notes on their pads, I saw . . .

Kristy! She was edging through the crowd, followed by Mallory and Stacey. In a flash, all of my friends were together. The hugging continued.

So did the tears. Best friends were reunited. The Babysitters Club was together again.

"Gosh! There were times when I thought this would *never* happen," I said.

"Us too," said Kristy, speaking for all the land-bound babysitters.

"Yes, this has been quite a weekend," added Stacey. "I wanted *so badly* to come back here and search for you, but Dad wouldn't let me leave New York till this morning."

"And Kristy and I have been out searching for you," added Mal. "We went out in boats yesterday and today."

"Bart and I had a huge fight about that, believe it or not," added Kristy.

"I *wanted* to search," said Jessi, "but Aunt Cecelia wouldn't let me. She came to stay with Squirt and me when we found out that Becca had disappeared. Then Mum and Dad came home—and Aunt Cecelia stayed. She's a pain . . . in . . . the . . . neck!"

"I wanted to search, too," said Mary Anne, "but I was just too upset about the fight I'd had with you, Dawn."

That was when I realised that every one of the BSC members had a different story to tell about this weekend. It was also when I decided that those stories should be written down so that I'd have a record of them.

A reporter stuck a microphone in front of my

face just then, but I'd barely had time to tell her my name when the director of the community centre stepped into the crowd with Stoneybrook's mayor.

The director held up his hands. "May I have your attention, please?"

Flashbulbs flashed. Tape recorders clicked on. TV cameras were rolling.

"We have two heroes here," said the director loudly, "Dawn Schafer and Claudia Kishi. They are credited with responsibly caring for four younger children, including Jamie Newton, who we have learned is quite ill. Mayor?"

The mayor pulled Claudia and me next to her. We stood side by side, as the crowd drew back a little, leaving us in the centre of a circle of admirers.

"These two young women," said Mayor Keane, "are to be praised for keeping their heads in a difficult, even traumatic, situation."

I think the mayor would have continued speaking, especially since the press was there and she was up for re-election, but Dr Weber nervously interrupted things.

"I'm sorry," she said, "but I want everyone of these children to come to hospital now."

"Me?" I exclaimed. "Go to hospital? Why?"

"I just want you and the others to be checked over. You've had a rough couple of days without much to eat."

186

"But I'm fine," I protested. "I want to go home."

"I'm sure you'll be able to go home in a couple of hours," Dr Weber assured me.

Reluctantly, Claud, Becca, Haley, Jeff, and I allowed ourselves to be ushered out of the spotlight to our parents, who were waiting to drive us to the hospital. (Jamie and his parents had gone ahead in an ambulance.)

" 'Bye!" I called to my friends. "I'll talk to you later."

Mum and Richard had to shield Jeff, me, and even Mary Anne from reporters as we left the community centre and headed for our car. I felt like a celebrity. But mostly I was glad to be on my way *home*.

23rd CHAPTER

The Baby-sitters Club

Friday.

This is our first official post-disaster BSC meeting. I don't usually write up normal meetings, but Dawn wanted me to write this up for some reason. She hasn't said why — only that she'll tell us later.

First of all we missed our Wednesday meeting. It's been a long time since we've missed a meeting. But we've had a good reason. And we didn't let our clients down, either. We borrowed the Kishis' answering machine, attached it.

to Claud's phone, and changed the message so that it said: "Hello, you have reached the head-quarters of the Baby-sitters Club. We can't come to the phone today, Wednesday, from five-thirty until six, but we'll be back at our post on Friday, as usual. If you want to arrange for a babysitter please leave your name, number, and a message after the signal, and Claudia will get back to you as soon as possible. Thank you." Then each of us said our names. We had solved the problem pretty well.

Anyway, we didn't conduct a very official meeting on Friday. That was because we were too busy talking about what we'd been doing on Wednesday during club meeting time....

189

Dawn

Mary Anne didn't know it yet, but the reason I'd asked her to take notes about the meeting was to help me write about our adventure. I wanted a record of the whole adventure—from the events leading up to it, to the aftermath. And Friday was just about the end of things except, of course, that no club member, especially the two of us who'd been stranded on the island, would ever really be quite the same again.

Friday's meeting began earlier than most other meetings. This wasn't because Kristy had asked us to arrive early. We just turned up by about 5:15 instead of later. We'd been spending an awful lot of time together since Claud and I had got back.

Mary Anne and I were the first to arrive.

"Hi!" we greeted Claudia.

"Hi!" she replied. "Have you seen the paper yet?"

"No. Is the story out already?"

"Special edition," said Claud, grinning.

"Where is it?" I shrieked.

"I'm not telling. I'm saving it for the beginning of the meeting."

"Oh, no! You can't! That's not fair! I'll *die* waiting."

"You've only got about fifteen minutes to go. Anyone who's been stranded on an island for forty-eight hours can wait fifteen minutes in my nice, cosy bedroom. Come on. I'll even feed you. I've got plenty of stuff here."

190

Claud began rummaging around under her bed and her cupboard. She emerged with Hula Hoops for herself and Mary Anne, and crackers for me. "Sit down," she told me.

Easier said than done. Especially when I realised something. "*You've* read the paper already, haven't you?"

"No," said Claud.

"Come on! How could you have the article and not read it?"

"I just did, that's all. I saw the headline . . . and I hid the paper."

"Oh, *please* just tell us what the headline says."

Claudia gave in. "Oh, all right. The headline says: 'Connecticut Disaster Victims Tell Their Story'."

"Wow!" whispered Mary Anne. "That *is* dramatic!"

A few moments later, Stacey arrived. Then Mal, Jessi, and Kristy. It still wasn't 5:15.

"The article's out!" I announced as each club member arrived.

As soon as Kristy had settled herself in the director's chair and was wearing her visor, I said, "Okay, Claud. We're all here."

Claudia left the room and came back a few moments later with the *Stoneybrook News*. "I hid it in Janine's room," she explained.

She spread the paper open on her bed. We'd made the *front page*! The letters in the headline

191

were each about two inches tall. They took up half the page. I'd never seen anything like it. And as I read the story, I thought back to how it had come about.

On Monday, after our rescue, we were driven to hospital. (Well, except for Jamie, who'd gone in the ambulance.) We didn't have to stay long. There wasn't much wrong with any of us. Haley was sunburnt, despite the mist and our efforts to keep ourselves covered with suntan oil. Jeff had cut his foot and not said anything about it and now the bottom of his foot was slightly infected. We were all rather hungry, although no one could say we were starving. We weren't dehydrated, thanks to Claud's rain collector. We *were* tired, both physically and emotionally. To be perfectly honest, none of us smelled very nice. And we'd been exposed to Jamie, who had a throat infection as well as an ear infection, but whether we'd caught anything from him remained to be seen. (So far, none of us has.)

We were home in time for late dinners with our families that night. (Except, once again, for Jamie, who was spending the night in hospital, just to be on the safe side.)

The next day was Tuesday. School started again, but the castaways were allowed to stay at home and rest. Jeff was supposed to have flown back to California the night before, but he went back late on Tuesday afternoon instead. And early on Tuesday afternoon, Jamie came home from hospital. Claudia, Haley, Becca, Jeff, and I were there to meet him. (Okay, so we didn't rest *that* much.) We were sitting on the Newtons' front porch when their car drove up.

The five of us jumped to our feet.

"Hi, Jamie!" we called. "Welcome home!"

Mrs Newton, smiling, climbed out of the car, carrying Lucy. I fully expected Mr Newton to pick up Jamie and carry *him*, but Jamie bounced out of the car, wearing a brand-new outfit, his hair freshly washed and slicked back, and ran to his fellow disaster victims.

"Slow down, Jamie!" warned Mr Newton.

But Jamie was feeling too good to slow down.

"Hi, I'm fine now!" exclaimed Jamie. "My throat's better and my ear's better and my temperature's almost gone."

"Jamie, you're not *completely* well," spoke up Mrs Newton. "Remember what the doctors told you."

"Oh, yes. To rest and take my medicine. When can I stop resting?"

"When your temperature has been normal for twenty-four hours—one day."

Jamie sighed. "Okay." But then he grinned.

So did we. It's hard to describe the way the six of us felt. Those two days we'd spent on the island had seemed a lot longer, and we were more comfortable together than apart, no matter how

193

much we appreciated being back with our families again.

On Tuesday evening, just after Mum and Richard and I had got back from taking Jeff to the airport, the phone rang.

Richard answered it. He rolled his eyes, cupped his hand over the phone and whispered to us, "Another reporter." But then he said (in his ordinary voice), "Oh, the *Stoneybrook News* . . . The mayor? . . . TV?"

"TV?" I squeaked. "What is it?"

"A press conference," Richard whispered.

Believe it or not, an actual press conference was arranged for the next day. Everyone wanted to interview the survivors of the *Connecticut Disaster*, and this seemed a good way to do it. We would talk to all the reporters and newscasters at once. Besides, Claud and I were *dying* to be on TV, and if we could arrange it, we wanted to get the other members of the BSC on TV and in the papers with us.

We were sorry that Jeff couldn't be here for the press conference, but Jamie was well enough to attend, so that was good. The conference was held at—where else?—the community centre. Our families came with us, as well as Kristy, Stacey, and Mal. And Claud and I insisted they stand with our families. We decided we'd use our influence!

194

The community centre was an amazing sight. Just like on Monday, after we were rescued, there were cameras and reporters galore, but since they were crammed into one room, there seemed to be even more of them.

Nearly everyone was interviewed, but the disaster victims did most of the talking. The mayor presented us all with medals for bravery. She had one for Jeff, too, which she was going to send him personally. The local news covered our story that night, but they had warned us that they only had time for a five-minute slot. That was pretty exciting, but what we'd all been waiting for was the giant newspaper article (with lots of pictures) that we'd been promised.

We saw it, of course, at our Friday club meeting.

"What does it say? What does it say?" cried Mary Anne. "Do they quote me anywhere? Where's my picture?"

"*Your* picture?" I retorted. "You weren't even on the island." Then I caught myself and added, "Sister dear."

The article was pretty impressive. It took up most of what was left of the front page below the enormous headline. Then it was continued inside. That was where the photos were—a whole page of them. There was a picture of the disaster victims, a picture of Mary Anne and me hugging, and, lo and behold, a picture of the BSC members!

195

"Ooh," said Stacey. "I know. Let's each cut out this picture from our own copies of the paper, frame the pictures, and hang them in our bedrooms."

"Great idea," said Kristy. "Hey! This article is a good advertisement for the club!"

Well, by this time it was twenty to six. Kristy hadn't called us to order or anything. We got two job calls, but Mary Anne just hastily arranged babysitters. Then we went back to the article.

"I feel like a hero. I mean, a heroine," said Claudia.

"Me, too," I admitted.

"Hey!" exclaimed Claud. "I've just thought of something."

"What?" I asked.

"We never finished our sailing race. We're still tied, Schafer. We still need a replay. How about it?"

I laughed. I knew Claud was teasing. "No way!" I told her. "No way!"

EPILOGUE

Dawn

And so our island adventure was over — except that it would never really be over because I would never forget it. I've written my story using notes from club meetings, diary entries, Stacey's letter to her father, and a lot of notes that Claud and I made when we got back. I filled in the cracks by interviewing my friends with a tape recorder. Here are final comments from the seven of us:

Claudia—"I never realised I was clever till I got stuck on that island. Okay, I'm not book-clever like Janine, but I'd rather be practical, anyway. It's too bad that you don't get tested for practicality at school. Hey, Dawn, I *still* demand a replay!"

Kristy—"I know I'm no shrinking violet, but I'm glad I stood up for what I believed in last weekend. I'm glad I cancelled the Krushers' practice and the game. Searching was more important. But I did learn that when you stand up for yourself, you have to be mature about it."

Stacey—"You lot forced me to see that it *is* possible to push your parents around. (Only joking!) The weekend was . . . I don't know. I realised how tied I am to Stoneybrook now. I grew up in New York, but Stoneybrook is definitely my home. And you're all part of my family."

Jessi—"If Aunt Cecelia stays a second longer I'm going to scream. Why hasn't she gone home yet? You and Claud must know how much I worried about you. But one thing I learned about this weekend is that adults in my family don't trust me as much as I thought they did."

Me—"I'm going to try hard to be the laid-back kind of person everyone thinks I am. But I suppose I need to know that there are some situations I can't handle as well as others. I've got limits like everyone else."

Mallory—"I'm glad I was able to help last weekend. Even though our searching turned up what looked like the worst clue of all, I found that I like to be active. It helps me feel in control."

Mary Anne—"You know I hate tape recorders, Sis. I can't be myself . . . What? . . . This thing's already on? . . . Um, well, here's how I read the situation . . . Talk normally? . . . All right . . . All right. This weekend was probably the worst of my life. I know that becoming stepsisters wasn't easy, but when I thought I'd lost you, I felt as though I'd lost me, too. I love you, Sis."

Here are a few final bits of information that helped me put the story of the disaster weekend together.

Dear Stacey,
  Thank you for your letter. I'm sure it wasn't easy to write, and I'm happy that you decided to send it anyway. By now, you probably know that your mother and I had a chat. Stacey, we'll try our hardest not to put you in the middle anymore. We don't mean to do that. And what if I also try to

199

Dawn

be more flexible
about which weekends
you spend in New York
and which ones you
spend in Stonybrook?
You're right. Your time
is yours! Also, from
now on, I'll remember what
you said about being a
divorced kid. I hadn't
looked at your situation
quite that way, but it's a
good way to describe it,
and it puts things in
perspective for me.
                    Lots of love,
                              Dad

Dear Mum, Dawn, Richard,
    and Mary Anne,
    I got home safely. The plane trip was
fun. Even though I fell asleep and
missed the food. Now I'm back at school
but hardly anybuddy believes what
happenned to me. Can you send a copy
of the newspaper artikle out here please.
                    Love,
                        Jeff

Dear Rebecca,
I hope you have recovered from your misadventure. I think of you and Jessica and your brother often. Are you sleeping well? Your father tells me you are back at school again, so that is surely a good sign. I am still thinking of returning to Stoneybrook permanently, so perhaps I shall see you soon.

(The letter goes on, but it's really, really boring.)

Best,
Your Aunt Cecelia

Dear Claudia and Dawn,
Thank you for taking care of me on the island.

Love, JAMIE

I suppose all I need to add here is a quote from one of my favourite films: "There's no place like home!"

201